LORETICUS

LOST EMPEROR TRILOGY

BOOK I

LORETICUS

J.B. LUCAS

First published in Great Britain in 2017 by J.B. Lucas
via Type & Tell

A CIP catalogue record for this book is available from the British Library

ASIN 1787450252

Type & Tell

ABOUT THE AUTHOR

J.B. Lucas has lived and studied in eight different countries so far. Passionate about high politics, he studied the inner workings of the European Union as an undergrad with a view to eventually working in the arena of international border disputes. His career has taken a different route, but he is still writing about the obsession that has captivated him his entire life – the tectonic movements of states.

He now resides in the darkest depths of leafy West London, where he writes using the inspiration of the India–Pakistan split, the founding of Israel, the identity crisis of Brexit and the maelstrom within the EU.

Loreticus is his debut novel.

Chapter 1

The priest stood alone in the chapel, calling prayers to a congregation that had fled and would never come home. He snapped wrists as he chimed the hand bells in an ancient rhythm, shooting their peals through sunlit dust in to the deep, cool corners.

Round notes bounced out of the temple's open doors, hitting the wood and brick of the cooling buildings in the dusk. They continued, muffled now, down the broken-toothed path of the alleyway, which stood as a dark frame to the glowing palace, basking with its height and age in the last half hour of the sun. Tonight a dozen killers listened for the bells and quietly moved into place. The priest, with his ageless call to prayer, was unwittingly signalling for a massacre to begin.

Thus most normal evenings settled across the capital, and shutters clacked shut as cool breezes came to disturb sleeping children. Old soldiers, now lamp lighters, limped down dry streets, leaning on sun-hot bricks to ignite the braziers on corners. Visitors would comment that the lights seemed premature, extravagant in the still golden light. But the locals knew how quickly the sun fell behind the mountains and how hurriedly the shadows and cold flooded in like a breaking wave.

The district around the Red Palace was a marketplace, crammed with ancient family stalls. At this time of evening they were all noiseless, the fruit stamped into the ground for flies and mice to feast on, the blood from the butchers driving up a briny smell, which hung in the nostrils.

Behind the painted towers and the high, crenellated corners of the palace loomed those black-purple clouds on the mountains. On a particularly haunted night you might see a flick and a flash of lightning, but the sound and the moisture never made its way to the capital. This was a dry land, a dusty land, and its people were not meant for the damnation smudged into those peaks.

Of the many active soldiers who roamed the quiet streets of the wealth-crusted city, none were more imposing than the royal guard. They were off duty that night as the young emperor was safely behind the steep walls of the palace. Many were eating or laughing with their families. Others were out, draped in no more than a tunic and carrying nothing more fearsome than a regimental dagger. The streets had been safe for ten years, since the expulsion of the zealot insurgents, and the population had short enough memories.

Statian was the captain of the guard, reporting directly to the head of the entire palace military. He was tall, elegant, settled in his own skin and was a man who bent the air around him as if his lean, thickly muscled frame weighed more than it should. He had fought in this neighbourhood every day of that dark year of civil war as the Butcher's men burned down the streets during the Terror. The temperature of those fires rose as the emperor punished the religious community, and the Butcher in turn spilled the blood of the empire's own soldiers across the city.

"Long may he rot over the mountains," muttered Statian to himself as he turned down a silent street full of memories. This lane had once been a frequent bottleneck of violence. Such is the irony of life that as Statian contemplated how each side had used this urban trap time and again, he was too far away in reminiscence to digest the present.

Without warning a hulk stepped out of an ink-black shadow, just as Statian's soldiers had done a decade before. Statian jolted into a sickly realisation of his complacency. The thug in front of him was too confident and professional to be a mugger, and he was too quiet to be anything other than a distraction. The palace guard turned hastily, the edge of his blade shushing as it drew past the scabbard lip. First there was no one behind him, then there was. From the side, a small ghost jumped and split open the veins on his elegant, unshaven neck with a whetted stiletto.

Statian knew he was done as soon as he felt the stinging, and he didn't fight. He wanted to nod at the man out of respect for such a professional delivery, but he was probably nodding already without knowing it. Humour, even in his last moments.

The small man stood back, his form unsubstantial against a failing sun and the chill dusk. He delved into a pouch on his belt, then threw something gold over Statian's head.

"Don't spend it here. You know what's next?"

It seemed the thug gave a nod, because the man turned

and simply disappeared. There was a shuffle, a wheeze and then a colossal grab of the back of his tunic. Statian, the tall and dapper guards' captain, was hoisted and draped over the thug's shoulder. His head bounced in step, blood ran over his upside-down face and his mind faded away.

Chapter 2

The Red Palace was a small town unto itself. Residential plots rubbed shoulders with administrative offices, squeezing the beautiful and influential people in to a space which, had it been less jumbled, would have taken no more than a half hour to cross on foot.

If a visitor were allowed to enter via the heavily guarded door from the market, through walls as thick as a house and as old as the empire itself, she would undoubtedly be important. Her first impression was of a small, perfect reception garden. Here thick-trunked trees sheltered the visitor from the late-morning sun, jasmine and lavender scented the air throughout the afternoon. Four grand arches, stacked two-by-two on top of each other, lifted the face of the entrance building which stared down as she walked further.

During the day the gate was usually open, or at least it had been since the end of the civil war. At the end of this simple antechamber was a choice. Take the left door and she would turn to the administrative heart of the empire, where hundreds of thousands of salaries were calculated, where maps were drawn, where taxes were collected and judgements given. Turn right, and the visitor would enter the important part of the Red Palace.

Loreticus's rooms were situated at the top of a tower in the important part. There should have been a warning sign outside his rooms, stating "Life is imperfect, and we need not accept this". It was a lament, not a criticism. If the visitor was unaware of this and on the wrong side of that invisible dictum, then she might be quickly dismissed back down the stairs.

If she had enquired about the occupant of these rooms, there would have been a mixed collection of opinions, all of which were right from their own perspective. Most ladies and young men found him charming, despite his fifty-something years. Children found him approachable and engaging, and servants seem to forget their subservience around him. But to be a man or woman of influence or pride in his presence was tantamount to a challenge.

If the visitor had anything to offer Loreticus in his work of defending the empire and its ancient ruling family, then it was likely that he would welcome her conversation. However, if the visitor truly did have anything of worth, it was more likely that a boy or old lady or run-of-the-mill merchant would have tugged at her sleeve the day before in the middle of the street to tell her that she was someone that "someone wanted to talk to".

But were the visitor someone of influence, it would be rare that Loreticus would face her directly, rather offering a gaze both direct and indirect. There was a sensation that he was always looking down from a slightly higher vantage point, despite his average build. It was nothing that Loreticus said, or implied, but it was a spirit which came over him. Legends were tattooed across his demeanour, telling of his deeds in the civil war a decade ago, and the bitter compromise he was instructed to make on behalf of the old emperor. The visitor might also feel there was ample opportunity to strike this man in his quiet contemplation, but the testament of his still being alive after so much turmoil offered the best counsel not to try.

And so Loreticus was in his quiet contemplation now, looking through a narrow window at a column of white bonfire smoke from the gardens. The window stood five storeys off the ground, and as such enjoyed a rare pure breeze, which touched Loreticus's skin in sporadic, gentle breaths. As he turned, his gaze came back into the room and turned once more proud and impenetrable. His right eye was still in the sun and stayed wide open, his left shaded and partially closed. This splitting of the man by the soft shadow spoke more to his person than any words could.

His gaze of vexation fell on his assistant, who once again had managed to hit a nerve. Pello was not a person that Loreticus plied his tricks on. He was not a threat, a man of influence or a person of interest. He was the quirky son of a cousin to whom Loreticus had owed a favour. He lived his life in lists, something which Loreticus liked, but his head often remained in some vaporous world when his thoughts should have been in the room.

Everything that morning was hushed. Loreticus's rooms were never a centre of rambunctious activity, but the line of bludgeoned and cold bodies that he and Pello hosted soaked in any fugitive sound. This silence was now sharpened by Loreticus's irritation. Pello had the talent of speaking when his master was just starting a statement.

"Gods be damned. I was trying to lay the logic out loud," Loreticus snapped.

"Sorry," returned Pello, pulling his face into a rictus of guilt.

"You always do it."

"Sorry."

"I was summarising our predicament for your notes. The emperor was allegedly with his mistress last night and now he's nowhere. His guards were murdered. We have no other candidate of royal blood. The thick-headed generals will have to take charge."

Pello always drew his thoughts on paper in the style of a knotted string. Each knot gathered existing threads and scattered resultant questions to the next range of knots. Loreticus looked over at his work.

On the left was a scribbled black ball with "Emperor kidnapped/murdered/runs away", with each option on separate lines. Underneath was "Bodyguards murdered". To the right of this ball and its options was a large blank expanse of paper. Pello scribbled a knot with the question, "Who's in charge now?"

"We have Ferran," offered Pello. They contemplated each other for a moment, and the unspoken rebuttal hung in the air as an unnecessary rebuke. "Why the generals instead?"

"Ferran might be my friend, but he's a lazy oaf. Between him, Antron and Iskandar, they command three of the four armies. There are very few men who have a natural authority to bring those scoundrels into line and so one or more of them needs to be on the seat. So better a partnership between them than the three of them squabbling," said Loreticus. "Our problem is that they only have the talent to destroy, not build something to last. If the generals go to war, it's a catastrophe for the country. But it seems inevitable. If the Emperor Marcan has been kidnapped, they have an excuse; if he's been assassinated, they have an obligation of honour. War would be the end of our empire."

He wrote the notes in his knot-map:

Ki•nappe• = war (ba•)

Mur•ere• = war (catastrophic)

Disappeare•/•runk = to be •etermine•

"I don't understand, sir," interrupted Pello. "We've always been very successful at war."

"Not this time. We're broke and we've got no-one nearby to invade other than the zealots. All our trade left when the religious community took it with them. So, it can't be the generals on the throne and Marcan has caused a scandal and disappeared. It seems that no-one is going to fix this mess unless we sort it out. No, there's no simple route back to where we were without Marcan in the palace." He pointed at Pello's paper and waited, listening to the scratching of the quill. He thumped the base of his fist in to his palm. "We must find him, protect him and return him to his throne. If he's still alive. But it still niggles me why Antron deigns to share the power with his rivals. I would have thought he would have taken it alone."

There was a movement of air in the room as a breeze found its way in. A newly mounted mirror caught the sun and sent blinding rays around the room. Modern décor, modern pains.

Pello had drawn a knot in the middle of the paper, with the title "Return of Loreticus's preferred emperor".

"Change that," snapped Loreticus. "Take out my name and put in 'rightful emperor'."

Pello did as ordered. Loreticus looked back out over the buildings. The phraseology was not an issue, he knew. It was the unconnected knots between Pello's growing cluster on the left and the solitary one in the middle. A lack of logic, and a lack of a plan.

"So strange it happened on a day like today," opined Pello, looking up and out at the sky, mimicking Loreticus's pose. The painted red stain on the outside of the building curled around the edges of the window. Clatters of broken speech lifted from the market in the street, the shouts of the traders robbed of their urgency by the height of the tower. He was right. The rhythm of normalcy sounded alien to Loreticus.

Loreticus sighed and sat down at his desk again. Three obvious possibilities to cause the emperor's disappearance, any of which would cause chaos. Either there would be war because of an assassination by the zealots; or a war because the three generals, Antron, Iskandar and Ferran, had assumed control of the throne and didn't know how to do anything else; or peace because the Emperor Marcan would be found drunk or hiding in a cupboard somewhere. Loreticus thought could he manage Marcan, because he was a deeply flawed man and a poor emperor. He could not help but believe once Marcan had understood the need for reunification, he would act on it. If the generals stayed in control of the throne, the threat of an impoverished country would cause them to race to ransack every neighbouring country. Another decade of war caused by shallow men who knew no different.

In front of Loreticus lay the wreckage of the slipshod palace coup by an unknown enemy. Slipshod, but still successful. He glanced at the mess, stood up, flushed his mind to clarity, and moved forward to the line of murdered guards. Throats cut, hair matted, skin marbled. He leant over the captain of the troop, someone who was well known in court and had even protected Loreticus on several missions. The old spymaster looked for a moment with compassion, then assumed a detachment, and once again went about a repugnant task on behalf of an oblivious monarch.

There were none of the heroic deaths frozen in the paintings around the building. This was simply a grotesque slaughter carried out by professionals on the orders of fools. Loreticus took a breath. He sniffed, opening his nostrils which had collapsed with the summer dust. He immediately regretted it. The air held a flat, gamy odour from the bodies. He didn't like the smell of mortality. It gave too close a connection to the animal world.

The long gash in the neck of one of the corpses had opened in a straight line, concentrating the colour of life into the inner flesh and greying the skin beyond it. This deep cut gave the neck an extra length and it gaped as the head rested off centre. This was the effort of a forceful killer.

"Professional work," muttered Loreticus as he walked along the row. He kept his voice steady whilst his stomach rolled. He wished for once his mind might master the horrific sights to which he was constantly exposed. "Four look like they were done by the same man and the rest by two or more who learned from him. The cuts are the same style but less exact and less deep."

Pello walked behind him, skin white and lips blue. His ankles wobbled as he made notes in his idiosyncratic way, walking and writing, rarely looking up from the papers. Loreticus could imagine Pello fainting during a haircut.

"Statian," Pello stated. Pello's quill had stopped scratching. They stared at the face, which lay crown towards them.

"Yes. Our friend Statian. Where was he found? Please say not in his house with his family."

"No, sir. He was left outside our door," said Pello plainly.

"Outside our door? Just here?" Loreticus felt his stomach constrict. "Five floors up? I didn't see any blood."

"No, there wasn't any. It was very tidy."

The spymaster was shaken. Normally Loreticus was the predator, the one with the might of the empire behind him. This was carried out by someone with knowledge, access and an agenda against him specifically.

"On that note, why did you have the others brought all the way up here? It must have been exhausting for whomever did it."

"Oh, I didn't want to have to keep walking up and down the stairs today," replied Pello without a trace of guilt. Loreticus stared at him for a moment, orienting himself to the idea that this was logic rather than laziness on the part of the boy.

"Well, I suppose that it maintains some sense

of privacy," he muttered.

"It doesn't look like Statian," said Pello, drawing his attention back to the face.

Loreticus paused, now realising the horrible newness of the situation for Pello. His junior's pale cheeks evoked his own virgin investigation of a violent death.

"Have you seen a dead man before?"

"Not up close," replied the boy. "And not in a room with more dead than live people."

Loreticus nodded and gestured for him to sit at the room's writing desk. He resisted an urge to rub Pello's shoulder in sympathy.

"Draft a message from an alias to Javus to ask whether the fanatics had a hand in this," he instructed. Pello tucked away his scraps of paper entitled "Assassination Investigation Project" and drew out a fresh sheet.

"Yes, sir." A pause as he scrawled the date and one of his master's spare identities. "Do you think he would tell us if the Butcher had been involved?"

"If he knew," replied Loreticus, and instinctively checked for anyone else in the room. "And stop calling Talio 'The Butcher'. I've managed to drop the habit after ten years and your repetition isn't going to help."

The row of corpses lined up. An acquaintance murdered and dumped at his door. These were ugly recurrences of the events of the civil war.

"It is uncomfortably convenient that it happened last night. Today I was due to meet the emperor and the generals to explain my case for a rapprochement with the zealots." He looked down at the row of bodies, willing himself not to check any were spying on him. "There's one missing from here. I couldn't bear to have him laid out with the others. A tall man with brown hair. I've asked the physicians to wash him down to see if there is anything we might recognise."

"Could it be Marcan?" asked Pello, filling out new knots on his large string of logic again.

"No," replied Loreticus. "I feel something inside me that Marcan is still alive. He has great tasks ahead of him."

"Bringing the country back together will be a victory, sir," stated Pello.

"Yes, it will. And I think this emperor might have been willing had he known the state of the finances. As soon as the clerks see we're running out of money, they look after their own wages first and the soldiers' last."

"So the clerks might have killed the guards?"

"No, you plum," snapped Loreticus. "But these two things surely aren't a coincidence. Marcan disappears, his bodyguards are murdered. That much is tight logic. Whether it had anything to do with the conversation planned for today is the crucial question."

"Why, Loreticus?"

"It shows who benefits. An unstable empire benefits the zealots in their new country, but simply killing the emperor benefits those who inherit the throne – in other words, the Imperial Cousin Ferran or General Antron. It's a ridiculous situation." Another sigh. "All I want is a peaceful city and short-sighted people spend their time tearing up maps."

Pello moved to the desk, scrawling a large knot between the cluster on the left and the one in the middle. Pello wrote "Who benefits?" above and put a column of dashes next to it. Loreticus watched him, knowing that he would fill out that list with names as they occurred to him. The boy's pale tunic glowed in the light from the window, making Pello look up again at the clear blue sky. Loreticus followed his gaze. The heavens stretched in their perfection to the mountains at the edge of the kingdom, the great looming slopes.

"It really is strange it all happened on such a quiet day," he said.

Loreticus considered him once more, then said, "Go and get changed for the reception tonight. Be back here in an hour with a clear head on your shoulders."

Chapter 3

The fashion in the capital was to hold parties timed precisely for when the sun went down. The light was hypnotic, a delicate blend of heat and gold, and the common philosophy was that this twilight calmed the spirit and encouraged fraternity between even the grubbiest of rivals. And so it was tonight, with the three vainglorious generals acting as a fraternity of hosts.

Loreticus and Pello arrived perfectly on time, when there were enough cliques to flit between but not enough of a crowd to get wedged against any one of them. Loreticus smiled, his perfumed grey hair styled tightly against his skull, his lips and tongue moist with a deep-red wine as he kissed wives, hugged husbands and clapped sons on the shoulder. He was in demand, and sometimes a queue formed near him as people looked to his stately figure as a safe harbour in the current storm.

Loreticus wasn't one of those guests who were cynical and half-hearted about an invitation only to remember how much they enjoyed company when they arrived. He was a committed misery and exuded joviality as only self-aware depressives could.

Smiling, smiling, he waded through the people, walking obliviously into deep conversations with a delightful comment irrelevant to any past dialogue. After each greeting, Pello corrected his clothes from behind, and flattened any lose hair.

Loreticus reached the end of the hall, sucked in a lungful of air and let his smile drop.

"How are we doing, dear Pello?"

"One-third of the triangle, Loreticus. Avoid General Iskandar, straight line to General Antron, a few nice words about how tall he looks, spin to the Imperial Cousin Ferran to tell him how funny he is, and then home."

The older man nodded, palmed his hair back above each ear and looked out at the crowd. From anyone other than Pello, these would have been words seeped in sarcasm, but the boy was deadpan and unfortunately all too accurate.

Antron was on the balcony, letting the falling sun lift the military gold from his cloak's clasp. He was laughing a little too noisily, moving a little stiffly and all round smiling too much. Loreticus noticed with a certain disapproval that Antron's cloak was the wrong style for the occasion.

Had Loreticus's late wife been here, his discomfort would have amused her. Now the recollection of her filled him with remorse. All these people were still here, populating the world with their chatter, their white teeth and togas and smooth hair, their perfume and the chink of glasses touching. The noise of blended conversations was overwhelming.

"Back at it," he said and wound up a momentum to start walking.

"Hello! Hello!" he called to the bankers and the doctors. He smiled so easily and so convincingly that his eyes closed behind his thick black lashes and people wondered how he saw to walk.

He glided past General Iskandar, who deigned not to notice him as Loreticus squeezed the hand of a chubby duke and took a hug from his tall, angular wife. The Imperial Cousin Ferran was on the third leg of his route, the one which took him back to the door, and when their eyes met there was a brief, not unwelcome nod of lifelong acquaintances. The three generals looked like wolves amongst these negligent sheep. Loreticus noted the way that Iskandar avoided any chance of catching the eye of Ferran or Antron. Subconsciously they had split the room and the crowd, who flocked to bleat around each of them.

"Normally it is a snarling battle with these three unchaperoned in the room together. Either there's an invisible chaperone, or I'm missing something," Loreticus mused to Pello.

"Well, they seem to be keeping their distance from each other," replied the young man. "Divide and conquer the masses, et cetera." Loreticus watched him from the side of his eyes. Pello's pensiveness either meant a question or a conclusion. "Could it be that these three generals came together for the sake of the empire in a time of need? Buried their differences and formed a partnership?"

"Perhaps," said Loreticus. "Their new camaraderie is certainly welcome. The question is whether they had any hand in the chaos."

Antron, content in his role of host, cut another conversation short to wait as Loreticus crossed the last few steps.

"So what do I call you now, Antron? Generalissimo? Emperor? Prince?" asked Loreticus.

"Good god, Loreticus, your small talk seems to dry up if the other person lacks breasts. *You* call me Antron, like you always have and you always will."

A moment in which Antron's eyes couldn't quite connect with Loreticus's. They were exactly the same age, peers from the academies of their youth all the way to fighting shoulder by shoulder every day during the civil war. But somehow Loreticus was settled in his skin, whilst Antron was still growing. It was this innate unease which had created a distance between them, and it was perhaps the bond between Antron and Iskandar.

"What a view!" exclaimed Antron, looping his arm around Loreticus's ribs. "What an incredible sight. The capital."

He opened his arms to encompass the great city which tumbled out from under the lip of the balcony. All roads pointed to the palace, with the grand, palm-covered main street, the corda, striking its mercantile path between the heavy gates and skirting past the palace one block away.

"Yes, I've always loved this aspect."

"Of course," said Antron, his smile undiminished, "You know this view well."

"I do. The old emperor's favourite place, other than his garden."

"Well, not many people had been here before we invited them tonight. There was quite a lot of excitement." He looked around behind them at the filling room. "Very excited."

As Loreticus looked out across his home town, a sudden feeling that Antron might throw him five or six storeys down to the flagstone courtyard made him turn with an unusual paranoia. General Antron was a clumsy creature, an oik despite his glamorous family.

We invite *them*, repeated Loreticus to himself with an inward snarl. He unsheathed a smile for Antron and opened a different conversation.

"Are you already moving in?" he asked, indicating the gaudy display of trinkets. The general had them displayed as talking points along the far end of the balcony, where he seemed to be receiving the worthier guests that night.

"I don't know whether you and I have ever been that close now I consider it, Loreticus," he began. His sharp Adam's apple bounced in his veined throat as he swallowed a decision. "I have a . . . prize, let's call it. One of the hardest times for me was when I led out my army against another tribe the week after Marcan took the throne. Another emperor, another barbarian. My life was repetitive to the point of worthlessness. Perhaps there had been valour and glory in my ascent, but now I was simply all-powerful as a military man. Of course, Iskandar is the greatest general in the empire's history, but where am I in those books? An easily forgotten peer of his at best. And then my view changed and I no longer saw the next rival as someone new, but simply the same man I had fought thirty years ago, just in different armour with a different army."

Loreticus examined the man as he hesitated before his next thought. He was a unique and impressive man, imposing, assured, and in any age other than when Iskandar stood near him, he would have been celebrated as a military genius. But to Loreticus, Antron only survived on one plane, that of battlefields. Perhaps they were incredibly complex and Antron's gift was in the deep, precarious strategy which had led him so far. Loreticus doubted it. Antron was a physical man who presumed that the tangible outweighed intelligence.

"Do you know my darkest secret yet, spymaster?" He watched Loreticus with his face partially turned away, as if he had suffered a recent slap.

"Your collection of skulls? All of the chieftains that you'd conquered, the men you've killed in hand-to-hand fights."

Antron raised his eyebrows and nodded with a strange satisfaction.

"Very good," he said. "Very close. I'll spend the rest of the night working out which of my most trusted servants told you. Is that as much as you know, or can you speculate?"

"A mountain of skulls? An ossuary with a mosaic of a map? A dining room kitted out with furniture made of the larger specimens? A suit of armour made from the bones of vanquished enemies?"

Antron laughed. "No, none of those, although I shouldn't pretend that they are all beyond me. Blood and guts and the pressure of leadership can scar a man inside, Loreticus. If you fail, I take over, and I took over a lot when you failed with the zealots. No, I have become an artist of sorts and my old enemies are helping me in my endeavours. Between us, we are creating the shape of my lifelong enemy." He looked deeply at Loreticus, wondering how best to explain, or perhaps considering whether he knew all of his secrets already. The spymaster's face was expressionless, other than a mild frown. He couldn't help but fear what Antron was about to say. "So I've had a sculptor build me a golem, a skeleton of my foe using broken remnants of my past enemies. The skull is that of a huge warrior I defeated when I was young, the bones of the hands came from an eastern lord who you might remember tried to challenge the family. His spine comes from everywhere, made up of knuckle bones, vertebrae, anything I could find. My problem was that by the time I'd finished his human form, I still had a dozen years and two dozen foes to commemorate. That's when I realised that he was a demon, and we built grand wings and a wicked tail. And now I've almost finished, but for the final piece. I don't think that I shall take to the battlefield again. If I did, it would be vanity not necessity."

"You've almost finished?" asked Loreticus. "So it shall remain incomplete? Rather unlike you, Antron."

"Ah, I didn't say that," replied the general. "I had been saving the tip of the tail for someone in particular and now it seems that it might need a substitute."

They looked at each other in silence, Loreticus feeling the pounding of his heart increase as he wrestled to understand the violence in the man in front of him. Even if he had seen the battles, lived the fighting, it was hard for Loreticus to put a shape to bloodshed, let alone identify the traits of a violent person in a face.

"Oh," he said abruptly, as if catching the thread of the whole conversation. "Am I the tip of your tail?"

Antron shrugged. "Not at the moment," he said. "You would be a good fit though."

"Antron," chided Loreticus in mock bravery, "you know that I've never been one for volunteering. Polishing up my punch bowl to wear as a helmet to war, no, not for me."

"No, to you the secrets of the lords and ladies and the tender exchange of coin."

"Indeed, well put." Loreticus looked around the bobbing and chattering heads, eager to find a change of topic. Something made him fear finishing the conversation in case it had repercussions with this madman that he hadn't previously considered. "Is Princess Alba coming tonight?"

"I doubt it." Antron turned to face the crowd, now looking in the opposite direction to Loreticus, but still close enough for the spymaster to feel the breeze from his movements. "If Alba did come, I'm sure it would only be to wish you a happy birthday."

Loreticus raised his eyebrows and turned his face to the general.

"Oh, you're not the only one with informers in the palace, dear Loreticus. Many happy returns! Should I announce it to the crowd?"

Loreticus smiled, turning back to look out at the mountains as the sun began to fall.

"No, please don't. If I wanted a public display of adoration, then I would have paid for it."

Antron nodded, steering the spymaster with a hand which turned into a clasp. The general's grip was like stone, cold, rough, unhuman. It held the chill of violence in each of his flat-ended fingers.

They turned their backs on the dusk-sunk city and to the wide opening which led from the pale marble floor of the balcony on to the chequered tiles of the room.

"Ladies and gentlemen," called Antron. Conversations quieted immediately, and a breathing hush kept the room.

"It is with immense pleasure that I should remind you that it is Loreticus's birthday today!" An impulsive round of applause, hundreds of eyes prodding Loreticus's face for an expression. "Let us all raise our glasses and sing for his rude health over the next year." He turned, hugged the taller man with a flawless gesture of friendship and led the crowd in a cheerful rendition of the traditional song.

Loreticus looked around the room, over the faces of the new people of note, the generals, their bankers, their wives and friends, the gleaming gold, the new haircuts and blunt perfumes, the clothes that were a little too colourful. And he smiled so wide that his eyes closed.

The room was fresh, quiet after the party. Outside a nocturnal bird whistled occasionally, answered by a distant partner his hearing couldn't reach. Loreticus ran his fingers over the smooth surface of the kitchen table, tracing letters and names in the fine dust. The sharp moonlight sketched the edges in the room, the plates and the cups on the side which the servants had left without packing. Pans were stacked, clay jars lined up.

In this kitchen, he was still in the company of Dhalia, his wife, as her ghost drifted between the table and the counter cheerfully, making the servants laugh, berating Loreticus with her wise humour, driving life and breath into every corner of the large room. She, her world, her life was never complete. There were always things that could be done to make it more beautiful and to prepare it for their pending family. Let her worry about what happens in the home, she had told him. His job was to keep her neighbourhood safe.

Dhalia had lost her brother and her father in the Terror, horrific wounds in a family which had been closer and more welcoming than any other he had visited. Even with this shadow in her mind, she had embraced Loreticus into her life with all of the risk and the blood and the sins that he carried in his role. She had ignored the worst of his deeds, instead celebrating the mind of a good man. He had always prepared for the day he would leave her a widow.

And now he sat in their empty home, a house which he hadn't slept in since she had died. His promise to keep the city safe was the only thing that stopped him from leaning his face against the cool wood of the table and exhaling his last breath. He would make her proud.

But he sat there, a deep and crippling emptiness behind his ribs as he pushed back the water swelling in his eyes. He knew that Marcan was dead, and he had lied to Pello to keep this secret to himself for just a little longer. He had seen the shape of the corpse, the colour of the hair, the shape of the fingernails. It was his job to recognise someone disguised.

So why couldn't he just join Dhalia now? Because he would be a failure forever, and although she would love him, she would not be proud of him. And with that small turn of logic, he stood up and wiped his eyes before the tears fell messily, and he closed the window shutters, and he left and locked the door.

The night was colder than when he had come from the party. The torches were burning and the two guards marched quietly behind him as they made their way along the wide avenue. He had a solution, but it would be possibly the greatest crime in the history of the empire, and he needed a royal accomplice for his plan to work.

Loreticus paced the lanes of the palace early the next morning, when the air was still moist from the dawn. He knew the layout of the palace in detail from the vantage point of where he now lived and worked. Hours had been spent poring over the feuds between generations of builders below as they scattered perspectives and angles in between the gardens and squares of the palace grounds. He could have easily walked to the princess's apartments through the private routes, trailing the corridors and the walkways. But today an inexplicable fear made him want to enter from the less toxic environment of the public street. By the door was a vast circular portrait of the Emperor Marcan, the sharp family nose honed slightly to fit. It had been carved at the start of his reign, two summers ago, before the constant anxiety stole his hair and left him wrinkles as payment. A tall, bronzed guard stood impeccably to attention by the emperor's face, and he nodded as he recognised Loreticus.

The guard knocked with the heel of his hand, and Loreticus peered through the keyhole as he waited. Framed against a pale vanilla sky was the dome, his own tower just behind the metal edge. This was the start of the reign of his third emperor, and the trend was downhill. He hadn't started with a high benchmark, but Loreticus now longed for those easier, earlier days.

Another guard, quite interchangeable with his colleague outside, let Loreticus in. They walked down a shaded path between sets of columns and under a grand arched ceiling, the floor paved in giant grey and white squares.

Then under the towering arches which formed the

terminus of other tunnels, and out on to a flat lawn which was peppered with gnarly, warped trees. Under one stood Alba, the princess of the empire. She was slender and tall, her hips cocked as she contemplated something in her hands. As usual, she was alone.

His footsteps must have alerted her to his arrival and she turned, dropping the leaf that she had been skinning with her nails. A smile played out across her face. Loreticus stopped, folded his arms and watched her fondly, admiring the way her eyes curved when she smiled, the way her lips revealed a little too much of her gums. She walked over to him.

"It seems that people always tend to leave us," he said.

"What can we do?" Alba asked. "He's gone, someone else won and if he ever comes back the generals will kill him. There is a healthy chance that they'll kill you too in the next day or two. If you don't get to them first of course."

They smiled.

"Sun, silence and happiness," she said with a broad reach of her arms.

"Well, let's see about that killing bit. You have your father's gift for paranoia and drama." He pulled out a chair for her. "Life is very disordered. Should I offer you condolences or ..." She shook her head. "Do you know what helped me through the last year on my own?" Loreticus sat opposite her. "Continuing to act in a way Dhalia would have wanted. I always wanted a glorious capital where people were safe and wealthy, and families could grow up without the fear of violence." He smiled, an expression which this morning was rich in disappointment. "I don't think that these three fools will help me to that end. I'm looking for a way to correct the situation."

"I'm surprised that you helped my father for so long then."

"Because he made a bad choice at the end?" he asked, surprised.

"Because he was a messy ruler," she replied.

"No, it was all to the same result. The generals know nothing about earning, only about taking. They'll bankrupt the kingdom within a year and we'll have a barbarian on the throne soon after. We need a wiser man in charge."

"Someone you can control? I have no respect for Antron," she said, in quiet tones. "I'm told all the fun people were at his party, and yet he somehow managed to turn it into a very dull affair. So who would you have rule us now, dear Loreticus?"

"Marcan."

She beheld him with a blunt anger. "You wanted him gone as well, and don't pretend that you didn't. If it wasn't for you and me, I'd have pinned you as the first suspect. And now Marcan is gone, probably dead, and you have no idea where he is," she said. "Anyway, he is certainly not deserving."

"We always think badly about the person running things. I know that you two were at odds towards the end, we need Marcan on the throne, but a more commendable version of the old one."

"Why can't we just find someone deserving?" she asked. "If my father had been the wise man everyone claims he was, I should have been allowed on the throne. But none of these generals are ready for that."

"No," said Loreticus, turning to look away. "They're

not ready for that. We'll find a deserving Marcan."
He pinched and twisted his fingertips together, as if
screwing something up. "Everyone thinks that it all hangs
on the fate of a single person– the king, the emperor, the
general . . ."

"The spymaster," she said.

He smiled and shrugged.

"If I brought back someone more deserving, would you
trust my choice?"

"I would have to, I suppose," she said. "So you already
think that I am a widow?"

"No," he replied. "I don't think that you need to be."

Alba folded her arms, crossed her legs and looked at
him. He could hear her mind moving, following where his
logic led.

"What a strange option to offer," she said. "I presume
that you expect my approval in that decision?"

He nodded, then stood and delved into a pocket.

"Do you recognise this?" He held up a small gold necklace
with a broken centrepiece; a significant sliver had been cut
or carved out of it and wings spread symmetrically either
side of the gap.

"No. Should I?"

"I don't know. It was found near a murdered man. I
think that it was dropped by a zealot. Ugly business." He
pushed it back into his pocket.

"Well, Loreticus, ever the cheerful visitor with a few
black clouds in his pocket. Tell me something to cheer
me up, and not something I already know." She examined
him quickly, checking that she hadn't been too insensitive.
"You do like the chance to wallow. Tell me something to

cheer us both up."

"The Lady Durring sprained her buttock with her lover. She told her husband that it was a horse that he had given her as a present and therefore it was all his fault. The poor man was distraught with guilt," he concluded, shaking his head. "I didn't know whether to let him in on the secret or to let him suffer as recompense for being such a fool."

"He doesn't know?"

"No, he doesn't. Nobody does."

"But for you and your minions," said Alba with a smile. "Which one of you was her lover?"

He was distracted for a moment by a gardener lighting a small pile of leaves. A fine line of white smoke rose unbroken in the air, whisked away where the breeze dashed over the palace walls. Something in the acrid smell had brought him out of the moment and he had forgotten what they had been talking about.

"How are you?" he asked.

"Sick of everything," she said. "I am so damned lonely. You know the old phrase – if life is hard, blame your parents?"

"Don't swear."

"Sorry. But I am lonely. At least when he was here, I was living in some vicarious fashion. Now I am both unwelcome and unavailable. I am the widowed empress and I'm not even twenty-five. Can you imagine such a curse?"

"What can I do? You know that I am completely at your disposal. You're my only family left in the world," said Loreticus.

"And you the same," Alba continued. "It's in my blood to

help the families of the empire prosper. There'll be a way for me to be involved before too long. Your peers prefer political fist fights to empire building. Just so pedestrian." She punctuated the last three words with a melodramatic flourish. "And what of your two little friends?"

"I don't call them friends. They are the people I have known the longest. And who are still alive. And life does go on for so damned long."

"So, 'friends' then. I don't know many people who like their friends. And don't swear." She took a drink and then fixed him with the same stern expression that she had used when she used to call him Uncle Loreticus. "So, we rebuild this mess before it collapses completely?"

"Exactly," he said. "Do you trust me?"

"Of course."

"Then be patient a little bit. I would do anything for this empire," he stated and drew one hand in a sweep which took in the hidden buildings behind the wall.

"Would you, Loreticus?" She regarded him. "Be careful of offering that. I'm furious at Ferran and his buddies and I'd have their heads on spikes if I could. Would you kill them all for me?"

Loreticus gave her an uneasy look. "Well . . . If the situation called for it, I'd do what needs to be done. You really can't ask those questions as the princess, even in jest. I really don't care for violence. It ruins my appetite, which is meagre enough already."

"Of course, I was joking," she said. "Anyway you don't kill people. You make them disappear. Much cleaner! Much more elegant, as befits the famous Loreticus."

He clapped his hands as if dusting them off

and smiled broadly. He said, "It allows me to keep my morality. What the eyes don't see, the heart can't judge."

Chapter 4

Last night's damp wood smoke sat in the man's nostrils, sending him an uncomfortable sensation even before he had opened his eyes. His mind didn't want to process the smell, pushing it away like a toddler.

Eyes scrunched shut, he rummaged around to identify the source of his fear. As his thoughts reached out, he realised there was nothing to touch, no structure, no memories, no name. The more he probed, the colder and deeper the void in his skull.

His chest tightened, his breathing quickened. A cold, stern fear bloomed inside his torso, denying him full use of his arms and legs. He lay paralysed by his own reaction, dead but for his rapid, dry pants. The fear rose, strangling his throat, cutting off the air as it struggled to his lungs.

The man sat up, eyes wide, sucking in a breath and staring around for something to repopulate his mind. Nothing. He recognised the smooth ache of bruising on his ribs, and when he drew up a blood-spattered tunic he winced at the sight of layered welts. With a certain amount of foolish pride, he realised he must have an impressive tolerance for pain, given they weren't the first things he noticed. The man continued to explore his abdomen under the dirty garment, seeing the long, clean scars from sharp blades at random angles. Most were old and flat, and the skin was elastic again. Nothing else on his body gave him any evidence as to who, what or where he was.

He got to his feet as quietly as he could. Unexpectedly he broke wind, then realised with a fright he might not be alone in the room. The fear returned and his head swivelled painfully from side to side, the spine between his shoulder blades rebelling with a deep stiffness. No-one was there. If fact, almost nothing else was in the room but for the table he had woken on, a few frames with pictures and a circle of sunlight in the middle of the space, which fell from the chimney through the roof. A sturdy door muffled various intermittent sounds from the other side.

He walked unhurriedly, noticing that his pedicured toes belied his thick-soled feet. A shadow of his face appeared in a beaten bronze plate, which he at first passed in hope of a mirror further along. But the frames contained nothing but cheap silhouettes of gods. He returned to the plate, picking out the shape of his face and his eyes and hair. He was tall, his complexion dark, his eyes wide. He had a bigger nose than he expected. How strange it was to feel so familiar on the inside and yet find such anonymity in your own reflection, almost as if you could choose to ignore it. His hair was short and felt clean, and he had all his own teeth. This presence of mind and judgement indicated he was from a wealthy family, he considered with a smirk. He amused himself at least, and he took his humour as a positive sign.

Peeking in the gap of the open door and the wall into the street, he saw a simple pedestrian scene which didn't look intimidating. It was time to venture out and to find help. He didn't know what had happened, or where he was, but he was sure there was a quick solution to get him home. He took a deep breath, opened the door and cautiously stepped through.

The street poured its people around him, no-one taking notice of this new entrant into their midst. His confidence slowly started to return until someone glanced up, then turned to stare. Two dark eyes rested on his face, their hinterland devoid of judgment and logic as they flooded with damnation and excitement. They darted to the wall next to him, then back to his face.

"Whore!" screamed an angry old woman, separating her from the crowd. "Whore! Whore! Marcan the whore!" With a swift step, she moved forward and slapped him hard across his cheek with a big-knuckled hand. "Whoooooooooore!" It was an animal cry, which echoed down the road. People stopped and turned to look.

He searched for what they were staring at. On the wall behind him was a vivid portrait of a man in his early middle age, with short curly hair, beautiful and elegant features, and a remarkably long proboscis. He absently touched his own nose.

"You bastard," roared a man deep in the crowd which was congealing around the crone. Spittle bounced on the man's lip, his fury kindling within him. He launched something with a gleeful heft. It struck Marcan on his right cheek, a sharp piece splitting his skin. It was then Marcan reacted. He grabbed the old lady by her arms as she came in for a second attack, swinging at his purple ribs. Marcan lifted her and threw her with all his panicked strength into the bubbling mob. She was so light she bounced off the taut belly of a merchant and fell on the cobbles. A shocked silence paused the entire scene. Marcan watched her, lying crumpled on the floor. The mob gaped at her, mouths open.

"Whoooooore!" she began, pushing herself up using the strength of her wrinkled triceps.

"Sod this," Marcan muttered and dashed back into the hut as, like a damn bursting, the inertia restraining the mob disintegrated. Bodies started to cram through the small entrance behind him.

In through the front door they flowed toward the front door, the first attacker a round-eyed middle-aged man. One punch, two and he staggered. Marcan pushed him like a plug into the door, then dashed to the back of the hut, hurdling on to the table, and exiting through the window. He landed hard in a curled roll on to the slops and broken pottery behind. Footsteps sounded down the paths either side of the hut, so he twisted and galloped in the opposite direction.

In front of him, the edge of the town petered out in to a sweeping golden hayfield, its young corn looking tender amongst the dark soil. The noise closed in on him, and instinct drove him forward, his sandals catching rocks and mud, tripping him. And then he lost the ground, falling face, then shoulders, then back first, as his burning legs catapulted him over the lip of a steep decline. He was up running again, one sandal folded back under itself, the smell of mud in his nose, his breath frightened. Tiles and rocks had bounced near his feet as the burghers launched their insults.

Their voices faded, and Marcan was away. He continued to run, a nauseous cocktail of wanting to sob and needing to shout occupying the front of his thoughts. He fell into a trot, and kept going.

Marcan sat, nursing a bleeding elbow and bruised knee. Both had been incurred on his flight out of wherever he had been, a village now at a safe distance. A seed, from a dandelion or a thistle, floated contentedly in the breezeless air, and he watched it as it danced indecisively out of arm's reach. Marcan wondered whether it was as grateful for the warm sun as he was. He felt its equal at that moment as it moved to silent music, opposite an invisible partner.

Who the hell was he? An inherent entitlement gave him a strange sense of purpose. But until that moment, he was insubstantial to everyone. Perhaps he represented a stain in the society. Nothing occurred to him, nothing felt familiar. Thirsty, hungry, bruised, dirty. These hands weren't his, these legs were someone else's.

He wasn't sure that he was a whore despite the old woman's conviction. He must have been a particularly bad one to have fuelled such anger. He didn't *feel* like a whore but then he didn't relate well at all to this rumpled body. He tidied his hair distractedly, as if it were an old habit.

Marcan stood, unfolding a body of strange proportions, and brushed the dust from the butt of his tunic. Birds that had been shouting at each other in the branches stopped, and a sense of dread came back to him. Slowly, he turned to walk as his ears and his eyes strained open. He heard a deliberate noise behind him and turned to see a pair of richly dressed horsemen, faceless behind polished helmets, their pendulous cavalry swords already drawn, move their mounts gently around the bend of the road. Marcan watched the shadows in the eye holes, hoping for some sign. Immediately he was prey again, and his mind switched off. His stomach and legs tensed, he crouched slightly and lurched as the two soldiers dug in their heels, snapping their mounts into a practised charge.

With alien reactions taking control, Marcan swung down, seized one of the heavy sandstone blocks edging the road, and spun, wheeling the rock at his attackers. Its trajectory was not at the first rider, who could have ducked or dodged, but rather at his heavily blinkered horse. With a terrific crack, it battered the bridge of the animal's nose and sent it into a silent stumble.

Marcan ran at the other rider, feinted, ducked and rolled past him and leapt on to the injured mount, landing shoulder-first on to its bloodied face. Down it went, trapping its rider's leg. Marcan clambered over the horse's shoulder, pinning the soldier's wrist and his long blade, and reached with his other hand, pushing a finger through one eyehole, feeling the disgusting resistance to his probe, driving home his dirty fingernail. The soldier roared in pain, dropping his sword and scrabbling at Marcan's hand.

But Marcan was away, quickly on to the loose weapon. The other rider had turned and was contemplating with some indecision how to help his colleague.

Marcan stood, dragging the cavalry sword in the dirt behind him, taking a position on the open road. The rider didn't wait now, spurs into the haunches of his mount, yelling encouragements as he levelled the tip of his own weapon along the horse's neck in the direction of his target.

Again, Marcan feinted, whipping the heavy blade with an incredible dexterity across the galloping legs, severing ankles, breaking bones. An animal scream, a human shout, and the second rider fell, cascading on top of his associate with a bang of metal-on-metal. Marcan walked over, eying the scene, and then dumped the tip of the steel blade clinically through the hearts of both soldiers and both horses. He threw the sword on top of the bodies.

He stared at the pile for a moment longer, dipped to remove the top rider's knife and money purse, and stalked off the road into the trees. He was alone and frightened, yet he held on with an ever-stronger grip to that feeling of divine destiny.

Chapter 5

All the way along the road, Marcan had seen small huts of a uniform architecture. His face was emblazoned on each, and most often the doors were open and the inside empty. As the sun fell behind the mountains and the air in the trees turned colder, Marcan crept to the back wall of one, a dark shadow against its whitewashed walls, his face pressing against the brick in mimicry of the big-nosed silhouette. He imagined the hut to have a homely scent of urine and old food, but when he stuck his head through the wooden doorframe, he saw only a clean pallet with a slightly higher twin next to it. The floor was brushed clean and flat. No animals slept in the rafters and no past inhabitants had marked their territory with a dump.

He went in, allowing himself to feel the chill of the setting sun at last, and slid the bolt on the door behind him. The system had been concocted to keep people out and not allow an absent squatter to make it a permanent residence by locking it from the outside. Behind the two pallets was a burnt circle matching the small hole in the tiles above, and then beyond the fire pit, a small beck rushed between the walls parallel to the road outside. It had been panelled by flat flints and was at once a waste disposal and a latrine. He paused, then splashed water across his face and his neck and then soaked his hair, careless of how many other rest huts were upstream. He took a deep breath, failing to match his divine purpose with this squalid end to the day. Glory might be his destiny, but the gods seemed to want to teach him patience on the way.

Marcan sighed, then pulled off the tunic, bloodied and torn, and crammed it into the small rivulet. Water poured over his knuckles and wrists, lifting over his arms, running on to the parched dusty floor, making an ugly mess.

Birds talked close to the back wall of the hut, vibrant and optimistic as he slouched on to the worn surface of the higher bench, falling asleep in the warm, breezeless dusk of the hut.

The tramping footsteps from the road outside popped his sleep. He lay, his eyes closed, listening to the various gaits of men and beasts crunch on the track as they approached the hut. Marcan slithered off the bench, slipping on the tunic, which was still wet in its embossed silk hems. Voices carried with the footsteps, and animals were rasping and clearing their throats. He sat, head down, praying they carried on past his door. He had no room to fight and no escape.

The pack outside drew to a stop and rustic accents started muttering to each other as they commenced their tasks, babbling to their animals to the clink of harnesses. A single rhythmic step came to the door, paused, and then hammered with something solid.

"I say," came a clipped voice, "I know this is none of your business, but I need to use the loo. It takes me a little time and causes me some embarrassment, so I prefer to wait for somewhere covered to allow me decency. I'm sorry to wake you in this way and with this request, but I have practised asking it many times over the years and it is the best way in the end." There was a pause. "Is anyone alive in there?"

Marcan screwed his face up. There was no peephole to see who was outside. If he didn't answer, they were bound to knock the door down if they thought the inhabitant was dead. If he did answer, he was obliged to allow the man his movement. He took a penny he had borrowed from a shrine the day before and flipped it, letting his destiny decide.

Without thought, he acted on its result, popping open the door, grabbing the knocking gentleman by the front of his robe and hoisting him in before slamming the bolt shut again. They observed each other, both as surprised by this sudden meeting as the other.

"Um . . . Balthasar," said the new arrival, holding out an old, muscular hand. He had thick, straight white hair, grown long on top and clipped around the sides, giving a youthful shape to his wrinkled face. Dark eyebrows rested above handsome dark eyes, and a straight nose led into a thick white beard grown just as carefully groomed as his hair. He had the air of a particular man, overly clean in his appearance.

"Marcan," he grunted. It was the first time he had said the word and it didn't trip off his tongue as he expected. He knocked knuckles with the man, trying to minimise the contact with his broken skin.

"I know . . . this must be an inconvenience," stated Balthasar with a slight stammer. "Latrine etiquette being what it is."

Marcan shrugged. "This is not my house," he said. "You're welcome to leave your soil here."

"Well, it is different in the palace," remarked Balthasar oddly.

"I suppose it is," said Marcan. They considered each other for a moment, eyes locked, reading the other man. "Do you need me to wait outside?" he asked eventually. "It's just, well, I might spend the day here and I don't want to accidentally cede ownership."

"Thus the rapid method of entry?"

"Indeed."

"If you don't mind my activities in your presence, I'm fine with it." Another brief moment of quiet, then a mutual nod and they went in diagonally opposite directions in the small hut.

Balthasar opened a bag by his hip and pulled out a folded wooden contraption, which with a flick opened into a stool with a gaping hole in the middle. He targeted it over the stream and then descended with his robes draped around him for maximum discretion.

Marcan slunk to the door, allowing it to open slightly. Outside he saw four men readying themselves to enter with force.

"You'd better let your companions know you're okay," he said. "Otherwise you're going to have an angry audience watch you pissing yourself from shock."

Balthasar called out, "All is well, gents. I'll be out in no time."

The group outside paused, then three of them moved out of Marcan's line of sight and he examined the remaining man. Tall, shaped by an outdoor life from his coarse-lined fingertips to wind-blown hair. The man's gaze turned, catching Marcan in guilty surveillance before he could shut the door. An expression of violence, frozen in Marcan's eye as the bolt slammed into place.

"They're a likely lot," stated Balthasar, watching from his folded pose. "They'd bust down the door if needed."

"I'm not going to hurt you," said Marcan.

"Of course you're not. Think you'd let me crap if you were going to crack my head afterwards? What a redundant statement."

Marcan eyed him. "Well, you aren't going to be started or finished anytime soon, so perhaps you'll die of old age instead."

"It is one of the curses of my years," muttered Balthasar. "It is a way the deities remove my smugness at living so long, by removing control of the most embarrassing activities. You'll see yourself one day."

Marcan turned away. He searched for something else to look at in the hut.

"Well, I intend to live a long life," he said. "And I trust the gods with my welfare, but a betting man couldn't consider my odds high at present."

"Yes," murmured Balthasar. "What exactly is your predicament?"

"I don't know," Marcan replied. He closed his eyes and eased the bolt open, edging the door fractionally ajar again. No-one was in sight, but voices came from close either side. "I woke up yesterday morning without a clue about where I was or who I am. I promptly got attacked by some old wench."

"In Bistrantium on the hill? Seems that she has given you quite a fight."

Marcan laughed, his first smile for a while. He turned to Balthasar, examining his knuckles and then lifting one side of his tunic to show his ribs.

"True," he said. "She liked it rough."

There was a disturbing sound of something hitting the water and as Marcan watched, Balthasar's face returned to a normal colour and his neck softened. He flew up and he scuttled down the length of the waterway, scrutinising his deposit as it travelled. He stopped, washed his hands and then stood, deftly collecting the seat with three fingers in such a way it folded in and fitted into his bag.

"So, what are your plans now?" asked Balthasar. Marcan's eyebrows drew together. He shrugged.

"I suppose I'll keep moving until I find out what's going on," he said. "Are those your boys out there?"

"They take their salt from me, yes." A pause. "They'll do you no harm if that's what you're worried about." There was a conclusion in Balthasar's voice when he spoke again. "We'd be glad to have you join us for the next leg of the journey," he suggested. "No-one in my troupe will allow you to get hurt. We're moving away from the capital and the next town is a good few days' journey, and I believe that I can keep you hidden for a while."

"Yes," replied Marcan, calmed unexpectedly by this gift from whichever god was holding his destiny. They nodded briefly to each other, then Balthasar bent to wash his hands once more. He looked around the hut.

"Travelling light?"

"You might say with less than the bare essentials."

"We've more than enough," replied Balthasar, now in charge as he squeezed past Marcan. He swung the door open, an action which catapulted the four men outside to their feet. "We've a new troupe member," he announced.

In total, the band outside totalled around twenty. Everyone stared at Marcan, one or two switching back to Balthasar as if wondering what had gone on during his normal morning stop.

"But he's ..." started one of the four burly door attendants. His voice drifted off as he stared at the newcomer and then at the clay portrait of the emperor behind him on the hut wall. Marcan stared at the man, waiting for the judgement.

"Under my mentorship and our protection," interjected Balthasar. "This young actor requires our company for the next leg of his journey and I think we might have a place for him in our performance next week. Anybody overly upset with my casting decision?"

The man Marcan had spied earlier turned to him, a brutish mouth rupturing lopsidedly into a grin with shiny teeth. He snapped out a laugh.

"Jed," he barked with a thick accent. "I'll be your Demetrian. You're going to make us all rich, I think." He held out a calloused hand and smiled.

"Samwer," said another man, older and with hair scraped back from his face. He wore thick eyeliner, his accent was educated. "I'm Loreticus."

"I have no idea what you're talking about," stated Marcan, looking at Samwer.

"Demetrian the imperial bodyguard," repeated Samwer, gesturing in the direction of Jed. "Loreticus the spymaster," he said, tapping himself on the chest with the ends of all eight fingers. Marcan's blank expression obviously didn't satisfy Samwer.

"We play the parts of two men who are involved in the court intrigues."

"Our troupe, The Psittacis, travel a lot because we're warranted by the palace," said Samwer. "Basically, the whole summer. A man could hide away for a few months if he needed to." He winked.

"Luckily, you look somewhat like your namesake the Emperor Marcan," remarked Balthasar. "Not quite as elegant or good looking, but we can knock you into shape."

"Why do you help me?" asked Marcan.

"These are chaotic times," said Balthasar. "We all help each other."

"And you're going to make us rich," laughed Jed.

Chapter 6

The small of Loreticus's back needed physical force to straighten it after the coach ride. He laid the warm palms of his hands against his hips and coaxed his spine up, pointing his rubbery face to the dry sun. There was the smell of ripe desert plants in the air, a citric and resilient aroma.

Threatening shadows had been running around the edges of his vision for the last few days, and he had taken to travelling under the protection of Marcan's old guard. If he were Antron, he would seize this opportunity by burying the emperor's influencer with the swiftest of stabs. But with luck, Antron wasn't as smart as Loreticus, and Loreticus's reputation still gave pause to even the wartiest of soldiers.

"Stay in the carriage," he muttered to Pello as he banged empty his pipe on the edge of the carriage door. The boy's hair was mussed on one side where he had hibernated against the padding for the entirety of the journey. Loreticus envied him and his pettiness bubbled to the surface, as it always did when he was wound up with stress. "By the way, stop using the word 'very'.

It's lazy. There's always a more appropriate word which I'd rather hear. You have been doing it again since yesterday." Pello watched him walk away from the door, then gawped around for someone who might explain what he had missed in his slumber.

Before Loreticus stood a brutal fortress. It was officially a guest house, but with its pocked mud walls reaching five storeys high, perforated only by the smallest of windows, and a single robust door which remained bolted, no visitor could have a doubt about its use. His servants were already engaged with the soldiers, offering documents and the bureaucratic disdain which was in itself as efficient as a wax seal.

Loreticus's entourage had stopped out of arrow flight of the walls. Around him the air was perfumed by the formal gardens, lacing the air with jasmine, lavender and honeysuckle. Small flights of swallows dashed over the land, harvesting evening insects. In the distance, far to his back, were the ever-present mountains, growing angrier and feeling closer over the last decade, their peaks snaring purple thunderclouds as they raced at the capital. The red fort reared up in front of them, staring at its visitors.

His servants beckoned to the carriage driver and Loreticus struck up a walk alongside it, his back now straight and responsive again. Within ten yards of the walls, the evening shadows had won and the air became humid and cold. Inside a huge door, a compact room with slits for murder, then a broad area for hand-to-hand fighting. Beyond that a reception room with polished brass and rare glassware. On one table sat a modest salt pot, half-full, suffering from age and impecunity. The fact there was a ceremonial pot meant both that she was expecting visitors and was still of some influence, Loreticus noted. The fact it wasn't replenished was the sign of her waning reach.

"I'd like to wash," he said out loud as he strode into the room. No-one had greeted him, so he addressed it to no-one. At his age, dust and dirt stuck in the lines of his face and brought them out in relief like an actor's amateur cosmetics.

It was a long time since he had worn the tight armour, and he never appreciated the reminder of the smooth mounds which had appeared around his waist. Even though he wanted to change into his dry tunic, he didn't want to expose his pear-shaped torso to a room now filling with military men. He settled for the attentions of his valet, who removed his breast plate and mopped his face and neck with a dampened cloth before quickly and unremarkably scooping out his master's armpits. Loreticus shrugged as if he were putting on a new cloak and continued walking, the soldiers of the fort leading the way.

Dess, estranged wife of General Iskandar, stepped from a shadowed doorway in perfect time to welcome him to the inner courtyard garden. Loreticus had seen her many times before but had only spoken to her once, when she married the famous soldier who rose from the ranks. That day she had been the bride at her wedding to Iskandar, the handsome and glowing battlefield genius and one of the four great generals alongside Antron, Ferran and Marcan. They had watched a parade along the corda of his cavalry, winged hussars and heavily armoured knights. A day ago, Iskandar was at Antron's new rooms with wine in hand, his handsome face rigid. Dess was now here, exiled as the mistress of a foolish emperor.

She was more regal than he had seen her before, even at her wedding. It wasn't a true elegance, one which was inherent in the bones of the person, but one observed and adopted. She had taken the sun, a habit which wasn't common in the capital. Her heavy lips were dark in now golden skin, her brows broad but perfectly shaped. But her eyes were darker, with an aspect of introspection which hadn't been there before.

A charming smile, natural and full of welcome. It surprised him before he realised that he must be her first visitor in this place of exile.

"My dear Loreticus," she said. "Please tell me you've brought me a few books or something else to read. Soldiers have such little imagination for conversation."

He found himself returning the smile of the most notorious woman in the empire. She was the lover who had caused an emperor to disappear. She was a legend, chattered about by the people in the capital, and used as proof of the empire's moral decline by the religious zealots over the mountains.

"I must admit I didn't think of books," he said. "One never does when one's surrounded by something in abundance. I'm sure I can leave you my travelling collection and suffer on the way home as a penance for my oversight."

She laughed. He let his smile spread, his eyes closing softly. Her laugh had always caught his ear at parties, but he had heard it differently. Now she was laughing from simple appreciation.

"Does that mean I'll still be alive by the time you leave?" A moment's silence. "Of course! You come to view the goods before you send your man to do the deed! I always forget just how professional you are, Loreticus." The word "professional" was used in a way only people of the court might use it–adept, learned, unnatural. It was a slight not a nudge. His attention instinctively flicked away, avoiding the long-feared confrontation.

Behind her, terracotta pipes ran up the walls to funnel the sparse rainwater into the underground reservoir. They were complemented by cypresses which echoed their height. A bust of a handsome ancestor of the fort's owners had been forgotten in a niche, overrun by blue flowers.

"Maybe my conversation needs practice," she said. "Let's hope you at least bring gossip. I cannot survive without that." A signal with her chin to her steward, who ducked into the shadows of one of the doorways off the courtyard. They sat on cool stone benches, his feet clumsy on the white gravel ground.

Beside Loreticus sat the woman who had hurt someone he himself loved. Her intelligent eyes watched him, carving out the jowls and the hairline, the hoods over his eyes. She was a polished character, but this environment, this boredom and this outcome had stripped down to the truth of her.

"How are you?" she asked. "You know you and I haven't spoken alone and in candour since you lost your family." It was said without malice or motive, at most as a connection. *Look at me*, she was saying, *｡oome｡ to ｡ie but not knowing when. Committe｡ for a crime of my own choice an｡ con｡emne｡ by my own lack of foresight. Look at you, Loreticus, the* *unhappy survivor.*

"Well, my dear," he responded in a dry wheeze. "This is a hard comparison. There is before, of course, and after. I'm only in the early stages of after. So, I have no comparison really. I'd say I was improving, but improving from a horrible place." The steward came, placed a tray of water, wine and cakes in front of them on an elegant table, then disappeared again. "I miss her of course, but I didn't ever get to really see my son, so . . . What can I say? I'm a lonely person who defends himself with arrogance and logic."

She leant forward to pour them each cups – officially his role, but he was preoccupied and he appreciated her diplomacy.

"Don't limit yourself," she said wryly. "You also defend yourself with a charming humour."

He saw her arms had tanned an even bronze and he felt a pang of attraction. It promptly humbled him.

"I can sympathise with your loneliness," she muttered, staring across the peristyle. "I think any true loneliness must contain a generous dash of remorse. So, I cover my regrets by focussing on the small things, the trivial problems. You know, the greatest irritation of this place is the lack of running water," she said in a voice from her actress's collection. "I've stared at this damned fountain for days on end trying to imagine what it looks when it has water. I am unsatisfied I will ever know."

"Why don't I see what can be done?"

"That would be amazing, Loreticus. That would make my days bearable." She smiled to herself. "You were always the charmer. Always the one who grants wishes to the ladies through a little connivance or a little influence.

Of course, you know how you were seen."

"Do I?"

"Loreticus, don't you pretend that it wasn't cultivated."

He laughed.

The material of her dress caught the hairs on his arm and he experienced a movement of heat from her skin as she lifted her wine. He hadn't realised she was so close. There was no seduction here, despite her tone. His presence was a reminder of what she once was.

"Do you know where he is?" he asked. It was time to play the hand he had come here for. Loreticus wanted a clear message to leak back to the generals. Marcan was alive and he wanted them to see his shadow everywhere they looked.

"No. I think I'd tell you, but I honestly don't."

"I wonder whether you would."

"I would. Not out of spite or regret but somehow as an action it might allow me to help rebuild the old status quo."

"No use regretting your actions because your coup didn't go according to plan," chided Loreticus, and he cringed at his supercilious tone. She wasn't a young servant caught pinching his crockery. "We all miss what was quite dramatically."

He watched her, slightly askance. Dess had always made it easy to be in her company if she wanted you to relax. At other times, when she lost her temper, a vulgar streak in her erupted. Even in her bright moments, the memory of her scowl coloured her placid features.

"I don't regret 'losing', you patronising ninny," she said gently. "I regret not appreciating where I was before this all happened."

"And where were you?"

"In love with a wonderful man, whom I have hurt and ruined. At the pinnacle of life."

"Don't worry," said Loreticus. "He'll be fine." He sighed, wishing the topic hadn't turned to this. "He, Antron and Ferran are now encamped in the administrative court of the palace, plotting and conniving. He's asked almost daily to see you."

"Iskandar," she sighed, smiling. Her eyes filled and she turned her head away from him. "It's rather unfair that I'm here and Antron and Ferran are there, you know?"

Loreticus examined her, trying to read whether she might offer the generals as conspirators to her scandal. "I always thought Iskandar was an honourable man," he remarked.

"He is, or was. He came from a very, very humble family. He didn't ever tell me who because I think they are still alive. How strange to be in that situation." She paused. "Do you know what breaks an honourable man? Not greed or ambition. It's pride. Even after his campaigns he had no money."

"Really?" asked Loreticus in a pitched voice. "I thought he was the shining example of the new man in the court."

"Maybe he is. The money he spent was mine. Any loot was paid back to the funders of his campaigns, or in tribute to the emperor. There's precious little reward in war nowadays. Unless you think invading Surran or one of the great northern territories beyond the barbarians is worth the effort."

"I don't understand," commented Loreticus. "What has this got to do with pride and honour?"

"He remembers every piece of luck that took him through his career. Every battle that could have gone the other way but for a mistake by his enemy. He's always been one campaign away from poverty. Imagine how Ferran and Marcan would gloat. You can collect money but it's harder to grow wealth. Antron and Ferran obviously promised him lands and riches beyond my own, something that was his and his sons', should they appear."

"So, what they bought was his loyalty and your involvement?"

"Too blunt, Loreticus," she groaned. "I'm not a whore."

He paused for a moment.

"I've made a lot of mistakes and helped the old emperor and then Marcan make many more poor choices. I'm a fool and a fraud."

"You're neither," she said. "You're a man in politics."

"Thank you for the wine and the conversation," he said, standing. Her sudden expression caught him unawares, a look of hurt and disappointment at such a short visit. His heart broke as he studied her. Golden blonde hair, young skin, inquisitive blue eyes, all aspects now of a portrait of sadness. She looked harmless. "You should come with me to the carriage. If I leave you boring books, then you might hate me even more once I've left."

She rewarded him with an honest smile which revived a thousand memories and thoughts of young romances in his mind. He turned, resenting the world and the situation he was in and the things he had to do. She stood, took his arm and escorted him to his carriage.

Chapter 7

Loreticus's meticulous consumption of detail was the spymaster's defining trait and his obsession. When there was a gap in his logic it worried his mind like a pest, stealing away any sleep or comfort. He had become pensive over the last year in his empty home, poring over puzzles and intrigues rather than the ruins inside himself. As his network slowly suffocated under Antron's reign, Loreticus felt these tributaries of information from around the empire start to dry up.

And so he took on the mundane tasks he had previously delegated. That morning, he had invited Selban to join him for the official inspection of Dess's townhouse. Loreticus imagined her walking in her grand prison, her fingers touching the murals or her bare feet on the tiles. He blinked away the thoughts. Unhappily he came back to the moment, walking alongside Selban and surrounded by his small entourage who stamped their boots into the cobblestones.

"Selban, I have an ethical question for you to

consider," he said. The boots of his guard on the cobbles made him raise his voice deliver each word, something he wasn't enthusiastic about doing.

Selban rubbed his hands together. The implied lack of morality would keep his attention sharp.

"There are things that I have done recently which I deeply regret. However, my regret is at the need to have done them, not at the action itself." He walked a little, looked over his shoulder to see just Pello with his nose in the air looking at the highest windows, and the guards ten paces behind. What he needed to say next was very difficult, and he kept quiet as he fought in his mind for the right words. He wanted to say, "Am I wrong?" and have Selban understand everything that he meant, but he couldn't expect that.

A bellowed command cut through his thought and made them both lurch with shock and spin around, their trailing soldiers marching past them. With an aggressive stamp of a multitude of boots on stone, a troop of the new palace guards turned a corner and marched swiftly to within touching distance of his own. They outnumbered his protection, their new livery of engraved silver blazing on dark-red velvet. Selban glanced back at them again and spoke silently to himself. The spymaster's soldiers marched slowly and stoically around their principal, hairs rising on their necks and their cheeks, ears painfully bending to listen for the scrape of a blade.

Crunch crunch crunch. The crash of nailed soles on to the stones drew tension up Loreticus's spine. He felt a loose run of sweat fall from his hair on to the nape of his neck, soaking in to the toga underneath.

He could feel blood in the air.

Ahead, guards in Alba's livery were waiting for them, swinging large fortified doors open. Twenty paces, less. Loreticus wanted to run and turn to face the thugs. Ten paces. Would they charge them as the troop wedged into the doorway? It was only wide enough for three or four men, meaning that if they were attacked as they entered, it would be butchery.

A loud call, and then the other soldiers were gone, turning away down a broad avenue, taking their sickly threat of violence with them. Loreticus heard a gloating chuckle from their officer. *Bastar*, he spat silently. He closed his eyes as they walked, all a little faster now that they could let their nerves act.

Deep breaths, damp sweat on the edge of his tunic. It was a horribly familiar shock, seeing an enemy with murder in their soul on these streets. He might have been a decade younger the last time he suffered like this, and still the fact both sides were native to this city shook his patriotic identity. A hunger was forming in him, and he knew that it would only be sated with a decisive and bloody strike on his enemy.

He pushed Pello in through the polished door which now stood wide open, flanked by white-faced guards. Loreticus took the boy's arm and guided him forward, resting a little heavily on the younger man.

"Find me that captain's name," he muttered to Selban.

As the threat lost its potency and his blood slowed again, he fought to resume a structure of thought. This was what had drawn him out on to the streets this morning, and this was now the spymaster's glamorous mandate: to hunt down clues for an emperor in his mistress's house.

"Do you think he will be here?" asked Selban. A little pang of childish joy came to Loreticus at the stupidity of the question, but it seemed Selban wasn't looking for an answer. Then he reconsidered. Selban didn't know what he did. His companion was not always a pleasure to be in the company of–and it was most usually just the two of them and Pello–but his knowledge and insight regularly astonished the spymaster.

"Let me ask you a different question, my dear Selban," he said. "Do you think the emperor really was having an affair with Dess?"

"Very possibly. Aren't you all?"

"No, we are not all. But if there was the suspicion, then why didn't Iskandar do something about it?"

"Disinterest, I always thought. Once married, people prefer parallel rather than converging lives."

"Not good enough."

"Well, dear Loreticus, if you were a commoner on the rise, should you attack the emperor on unproven gossip?" At times, when Selban was trying to make a point, he used a voice which sounded like a man straining at the toilet. "But more importantly, why didn't Iskandar seem more upset by the scandal?"

"What do you mean?" asking Loreticus. "Are you implying that he knew in advance?"

"Or perhaps he was in on it. He's moved from being a stiff-necked general to being one of the three men running the empire. He didn't come from the gilded folk," continued Selban, and he smiled to emphasise his point. Loreticus blinked at the food plastered between his teeth.

"He moved as far up the social mountain as he might have dreamed," commented Loreticus.

"I thought that Iskandar hated court life?" enquired Pello.

"I'm sure he does," remarked Loreticus. "But the generals currently need each other like the legs of a tripod. It isn't friendship which brought them together now. Antron the eager, Iskandar the meagre, and Ferran the monster. That's not fair. I do like Ferran. He loves anything that makes him laugh, and I make him laugh."

He stopped and folded his arms, examining the spacious courtyard they had just encountered. It was dry and well decorated in a bland manner. Pale tiles, pale walls, medium-height plants, nothing exceptional other than its size. He summoned up old phrases from Dess and Iskandar, trying to imagine their voices creating a home within the building. "But would he have given up his entire marriage and all of his dignity on such a gamble?"

"Maybe that's his way of getting angry," stated Pello. He disappeared behind a large shrub in search of something which had caught his attention.

Selban looked to Loreticus for a response, and Loreticus knew that it was a valid piece of logic. If Iskandar was being cuckolded, then this revenge was blunt and effective. Very much in character.

Their marital home wasn't built out of the red-painted brick of the modern structures, but from an older sandstone. It had an angular feel to it–a façade with once symmetrical rows of windows which had lost none of their impressive impact. Half-buried engravings climbed up the walls to a fierce entablature.

Despite its age, there was something out of fashion about the style of the house. It was too crisp, too clean in its approach to guests. The sharply edged front door led down a utilitarian corridor, its air cool and funnelled. Blind windows offered relief to the walls as miniature follies on its twenty-step length. Out into the broad, pale-grey stone of the inner courtyard with its trimmed plants and its flagstones beaten by footsteps into an almost single, polished block. The occasional servant glanced at the visitors as they performed their chores around the building, managing the family finances or guarding the vault until Iskandar came to claim his home.

"Tell me, Selban, why are the generals working together?"

The other man smiled. "I wondered why you had asked me here," he said. "I'm not known for my searching skills." He poked at a mosaic on the wall with a thick fingernail. "The only reason why Antron would do a deal with Iskandar would be to stuff Ferran, and vice versa. The only reason why Ferran talks to either is to incite them to hit each other so that he could watch. Iskandar I don't know well enough. I presume that he is the mortar the other two need between their respective brick heads."

They were now walking the perimeter of the central peristyle, where guests had been entertained in healthier times. Along the wall there were a dozen small urns containing members of the family who had lived in the house.

Pello stepped forward and started listing the names on the urns in his notes.

Selban peered at the names on the tiles and examined

the little pots underneath. "I remember some of these," he said. "Certainly, her parents and grandparents. Not hugely influential people, but humorous enough and they were always invited and inviting people."

"I'm sure they remember you fondly as well," remarked Loreticus mordantly. "How many urns are there in your wall?"

"Oh, not as many and not as pretty," Selban replied.

Loreticus was in the mood to continue to irritate Selban but paused in regret of his pettiness. Instead, his eyes moved to a familiar motif. He came to stand next to Selban and stooped slightly to look at the line-up. Each urn was ebony, carved with a small swift or swallow in what looked like pearl.

"Pello, have we been here before?" he asked, bemused. "I have seen this symbol before."

"Not to my knowledge," replied Pello. He drew a representation of the bird on his paper.

"And not with me," stated Selban. "Their parties were always at Iskandar's place. Maybe a letter that you received?"

Loreticus shook his head and continued to stare at the small containers. All of them were familiar, but he hadn't seen any of them before. A spymaster with a memory perforated with age–what a poor choice for the emperor to be relying on. He pulled a face of frustration.

"You'll work it out," muttered Selban next to him, his breath carrying wafts of lunch. Loreticus grunted, straightened, and they continued their search.

Chapter 8

The men and women in The Psittacis who came to the old man rarely saw Marcan, and their bodies tended to avoid him as if he were cursed.

He guessed that he had judged Balthasar well, but not perfectly. He had taken his white hair as a sign of old age but it was instead prematurely white. In the light of the morning, he could see a vitality in every mannerism in his face and the grace of his limbs.

The troupe leader laid out a map on a makeshift table and smoothed it with his hands. The beaten paper was waxed and creased, but the ink underneath was still crisp. Marcan scoured it for recognisable names or shapes, but nothing came back to him. He turned his head to see Balthasar watching him.

"Any comments?"

"No. But I do have a sense that I need to get somewhere. I have no idea where yet though."

"Anywhere to avoid?"

"Only here I think," muttered Marcan and pointed at a

settlement on top of a hill.

"The scary old lady?" asked Balthasar. Marcan nodded. The old actor slipped a flat crystal lens into one eye socket. Marcan stared at him.

"Are you some sort of magician?"

"No," muttered Balthasar, answering the question for the umpteenth time. "I was born with one eye from my father and the other from my mother. Both true eyes but they tend not to look at the same thing if left to their own devices. This tricks one into matching the other."

He slid his finger over the map, a pleasant dry scratch sounding against the dried laminate.

"This is where we are going. In a week's time, we shall be staging one of the old plays before they are banned by the incoming emperor, whoever he may be. We are one man short for our full tally but we normally plug the gap with a local. It tends to draw a larger crowd if one of the village studs is on stage. But in this instance, my personal gods have given me you and I'd like to wrap you into the role." No questions, no requests. Just a simple statement.

"How do you know what happens in the court?" asked Marcan.

"We're mandated to know. It's our job," replied Balthasar from where he was sitting, untying a bag in front of him. "We get paid by the palace to educate the country folk. Of course, we never stick to the script. If the emperor truly wanted to make his people happy, he'd employ better playwrights in the palace. I fall asleep reading what they send. Handsome pay for handsome folk though."

"I was right about you when I first saw you," stated Marcan. "You do like your own way." Balthasar smiled.

"Just don't make me want to throw you into that stream with everything else you left in there."

Later that afternoon, whilst Marcan had taken off to rest in the shadows of the forest, Balthasar found space behind the carriages, letting the team construct the stage and backdrop, put on their greasepaint and costumes, and to contemplate his luck.

"As usual, Boss, we find you sitting doing nothing," smirked Jed as he and Samwer approached Balthasar.

"I am not doing nothing, you oik. I am staying out of the way," replied Balthasar in his baritone voice. "What do you want? I think I can guess, but I like to make you work."

"What's the plan with the Marcan actor? He's similar, but not perfect," said Samwer.

"Have you ever seen the emperor in the flesh?" asked Balthasar.

"No."

"Other than the crappy clay portraits, seen him in official pictures or busts?"

"No."

"Then let me tell you, Samwer, that he's not just similar, he's identical. To the finest detail," said Balthasar. "His eyes, the colour of his hair, the shape of him. The only difference is the walk and the expression on his face, but I can beat those in to him."

"So he's a money-earner?" asked Jed.

"You're a fool, Jed. The question you should be asking is why Marcan is more valuable as an actor than as a reward we'd get from Antron." said Samwer.

Balthasar eyed him.

"Because," replied the older man. "If we tell the wrong person, we could be hanged as kidnappers. If we tell the ones with the most to gain from him not being found, we are most likely to disappear as well."

"I know someone who works for one of the generals. I trust him. Want to meet him?" asked Jed.

"I don't know. Which one does he work for?"

"Antron," said Jed.

"We'd be selling a man to a murderer with a lot to gain."

"We'd be rich," stated Jed.

Balthasar nodded slowly. "Talk to him and ask him the reward."

Chapter 9

Loreticus sat in front of a stiffened corpse. Despite his fearsome reputation, death and violence were infrequent tools in Loreticus's bag. He left the greater bloodshed to the warlords like Marcan and Antron, who revelled like harvesters in an autumn field. The vision in front of him was so horrific, he had been warned to come alone and he appreciated the advice now. Pello would have fainted.

The body had been beaten thoroughly. Twelve stabs across the torso, but the violence was most evident in the damage to the head and face.

"My theory is that they were trying to hide his identity," stated the physician, wax blocking his snoutish nose. "They totally destroyed his face. And they didn't kill him with the first few stabs when perhaps they could have done."

"Twelve stabs, Sempus. Twelve. I'd say either the attacker couldn't get close enough or the dead man was wearing armour."

"Um, yes, true. A well-brought-up grown man. Nice teeth, decent height, kept in rude health. Very few scars."

"Could it be anyone we know?"

"If you're asking, dear Loreticus, whether this is the body of Marcan, I have no idea," Sempus stated. He had obviously been hoping to avoid that response. "This corpse belonged to someone important, but I don't know who."

Much as Loreticus liked the physician, he found his penchant for drama in his work a little disturbing.

"No scars, birthmarks?"

Sempus whisked back the cloth covering the torso.

"Take a look – the body is so bruised that any superficial traces have disappeared under the black. I don't see anything that I would recognise."

"Did you attend on the emperor at any time?" asked Loreticus, watching the physician's face.

"No. He always used his family doctor, even for the worst injuries."

Loreticus looked back at the body and drew off the cloth until it lay completely naked on the slab. He leant in close, peering at the wrists and the ankles.

"I didn't see any military insignia," stated Sempus, slighted by the suggestion that he might have missed a tattoo. But Loreticus wasn't looking for such a mark. He paused as something caught his eye, stood up and pulled the cloth over the full stretch of the man.

"Burn him today," he said. "I don't want any rumours or gossip about this spare body."

"I couldn't get it arranged today," said Sempus, flustered. "The ceremonies, the pyre, the professional mourners–" His voice drifted off as he saw Loreticus's expression.

"I'll have someone take the burden off your back then. Two of my men will collect the body within the next hour or so. For the sake of the imperial family, I'd like you to forget that you ever saw this victim."

"Yes, Loreticus."

"Don't worry, Sempus," the spymaster sighed as he looked at the man standing before him, his apron spattered with blood, knives sheathed in pockets around his waist. "You're not in trouble with me." Loreticus paced back to the desk, where Sempus had started a sketch of the body to record the death. There was the bloodied tunic, folded and resting on the man's shoes. Three rings with dried blood sat next to the pile. Loreticus took the chain with the chisel mark from his pocket and held it up for Sempus to see.

"Tell me about this necklace that was found with the soldiers' bodies."

"Well, I don't know the insignia on it but I do know the jeweller's stamp," said Sempus, regaining his confidence. He had obviously been looking forward to that particular reveal.

"Who?" asked Loreticus, wearying of the physician's manner of relaying information.

"Magna the Zealot."

"Oh," said Loreticus. He stood straighter, the cogs of his thoughts clicking together as the logic took shape. "That is interesting. The zealots do have a hand in this. Is she still in the city?"

"She is, in fact. She didn't leave. Apparently, she says her god is everywhere, but we all know her client base is here."

Magna slouched on her afternoon chair, settling in for an afternoon's nap amid the remnants of a colossal lunch.

Loreticus watched through the window, seeing the fat old jeweller wiggle into comfort. The spymaster gave a signal and a soldier hammered on the door. Magna jerked up, then tumbled back with a scowl folding her zealot's blue dot on her ruddy face.

"Closed!"

The knocks cracked out again, rattling glasses and crockery. Loreticus smirked as she swore, rocked herself upright, and padded over to the door. Magna glanced at the imperial livery through her spyhole, then hurriedly belted her robe and pulled back the bolts.

Two guards marched in and glanced around the room before letting Loreticus enter. The shop was shadowed and smelled of cooling food. He smiled at Magna as if they were old friends and planted a kiss on her fingers.

"Madame Magna, doyenne of the capital's jewellery market," he said.

"Yes," she replied hesitantly. "And who are you?"

"I'm sorry, my arrogance is my biggest flaw. My name is Loreticus. I work at court."

"Oh, Loreticus, yes, sir. I have certainly heard your name. How might I be of help?" she asked in a quiet voice.

"This," he said, offering the necklace. "This is of interest. I understand that it is your remarkable work?"

"Yes, it is," she replied, stretching it between her hands and raising a curved, spattered lens to her eye. "But not really. I had a lot of people working for me before the exodus. The market was a lot richer then." A thought came into her eyes, and she regarded the visitor. "Didn't I sell you something once?"

"Honestly, I have no idea," he laughed. "But I've not been to this house before. Who did you make this for?"

"Well, it's one of my cheaper pieces so it was done by one of my apprentices. It looks like it had the crest of

Dess Oranti or her father on it, but someone has cleft it to try to mask the provenance. Part of a funeral bequest, if I remember well."

"Dess?"

"Yes, but perhaps never collected. This doesn't look like something the family themselves wore."

"But it still looks quite valuable," said Loreticus.

"Nothing I do is cheap, Mr Loreticus," said Magna proudly. "But cheaper things like this are often in circulation as unofficial currency."

"Why so? They are eminently traceable."

"Because the buyer has nothing else to give but can prove that it's valuable," said Magna. "You should ask those people who don't offer loans. Hookers, judges, knifemen."

"What a troubling life you must lead to encounter these people," remarked Loreticus. "And you just a simple artisan."

"That source of supply is where I get most of my raw material."

"Let me ask one more thing," said Loreticus. "Why did someone leave this at the scene of a crime? Isn't that a little blatant for a frame? Isn't it also a little expensive?"

"Left? No, I can't imagine that this was left on purpose. This was dropped by accident. It's too expensive for a simple stunt but if you had wanted to leave a clue, then there are cheaper options. Your suspect, sir, is a clumsy criminal."

Chapter 10

Marcan, like most of the people who attended plays, had presumed actors were in the trade for want of another skill set. He soon found that he was fundamentally wrong. Before the first day of rehearsals was finished, he realised that to avoid absolute embarrassment he needed to comprehend a whole new dimension. To illuminate a character, it wasn't enough to understand the role, but he had also to understand how he thought of himself, how the audience considered him and then to fit that into the play. The more Balthasar or Samwer told him to "just be himself", the more deadpan he became. Jed unhelpfully told him that he couldn't act like he was falling even if he was thrown off a cliff.

"Speak clearly, preferably the lines you were given. Don't knock over the furniture or anyone else. Get off when you're supposed to," he said.

He had never considered how manly or silly his own gestures were; whether they were elegant or brutish; what effects they had on other people with their hints of violence or calm. Extrapolate those miniature messages into the actions of an emperor, and the flick of a fingertip was as terrifying as a thunderbolt.

And so it was that he stood on a dry evening, his wan skin from a fortnight earlier now dark from the sun, whispering his lines to himself and concentrating on not releasing his bladder into his chalk-white robes. He was to play the emperor, married to the daughter of the last king of kings. The weighted hem of his tunic broadcast shivering knees underneath. The charcoal around his eyes felt sticky. He felt, in short, rather peculiar.

The stage was an expanse of wooden boards which they carried on the waggon. It was propped up by sandbags, and backed by a thick oil canvas with an imperious domed fortress painted on it. In front of the stage was a map draping down, with the mountains and seas and the names of what looked like countries and cities daubed. The whole thing stank of paint and grease, and it creaked with the slightest weight. In the daylight, it looked a poor effort, boards of different colours and lengths, the quality of the painting rudimentary. But at night, the torches cast their spell, and shadows appeared, along with walls and warmth and luxury.

Jed, who played his bodyguard Demetrian, oversaw getting him on and off stage before he fainted. The play itself explained and dramatised the politics of the subversive generals Ferran, Antron and Iskandar. They were unlikely partners, explained Jed. Their last play had been about the impending war between Antron and Iskandar, who had always vied for military glory.

"You don't understand how other people see the world," stated Jed with his thick rural accent. "Some don't like being under the yoke of others, some worry they are missing the chance to be great, some want to be better than their fathers. In Marcan's case, it was always rumoured that he bumped off the old boy after he'd married the daughter. None of these people are nice. None of them are like us." He applied a little more charcoal to Marcan's eyes. "Remember that when you're on stage - you're working to your own blind arrogance and ignorant of the generals' plots." He stood back and considered Marcan. Marcan turned to look at him. A moment passed. "If you're going to throw up, let's get it done, but cleanly." Marcan nodded and turned to a bush, and his food thundered out of him.

"Very good," said the actor playing Ferran from behind them. He was methodically lighting the torches to guide the audience when they started to arrive. Unlike others in the court, Ferran had honey-brown hair which he teased into curls to publicise his foreign blood. The actor was younger than Ferran, but his youth and his swagger gave the general believable dynamism. "Once you vomit, you know you respect the audience more than yourself. It is the sign of a real actor," he announced with a melodramatic flick of his hand. He laughed and patted Marcan on the back in mock sympathy. "Well, the potential to be one."

Marcan turned his damp face towards him, hoping they would realise that he couldn't appear on stage in this state.

"Too late," smiled the actor playing Ferran with knowing glee. "You're the emperor for tonight at least."

The audience was huge, numbering over a hundred. This was a unique occasion in the season for the village; the girls came for the handsome actors, the boys for the glorious military, and the elders for the gossip and the politics. They sat on the floor, some drunk, some impatient and all childishly excitable.

Marcan stood at the front of the line of actors as they prepared to file on to the stage for the introduction of each character. Balthasar was in front of him, waiting for the perfect moment to catch and harvest the audience's attention. He turned to Marcan, mouthed "Wait", then sauntered on to the raised wooden boarding.

"My fellow citizens," he started, "thank you for coming out to see our humble play. As you know, we are a troupe of actors called The Psittacis. We are requested by the court to present the histories of our great nation and we have done so for many a year with a deep sense of honesty, which is probably why it's best that the court don't see it! But this last year has presented some rapid change around the throne. The king of kings falls, a glorious new hero arises, only to be thrown into scandal, generals clash, and with each parry and cut, they see that the prize is the ownership of the world. But it is not swords that they duel with. It is lives and reputations. Fortunes and curses. They warp the fabric of the god-given world to meet their ambitions." His delivery was speeding up and he flattened his hand in front of himself as if to calm down. A deep breath. "So, let me ask your indulgence, if I may. We want to help you to understand what has happened in the near past, but we do so under threat from the court. Tell no-one of what you see here tonight. Do not let your family and friends in other villages on our route know, for amongst them there might be an informer to the court. Tonight's performance is a secret between you and us." Silence. Not a person moved as coughs were smothered and itches ignored. "Then let me introduce those involved in this terrible affair."

Jed gave Marcan a push between the shoulder blades. It took an explicit instruction from his head to his feet to lift off the ground and to start walking, but move he did. With each step, the stage was eaten up until he walked behind Balthasar. He could hear the flames crumpling the air around the torch as the crowd went silent to judge him.

"The emperor!" cried Balthasar.

"Boo!" "Faggot!" "Cheat!" roared the crowd, completely taking Marcan by surprise. He stopped and turned to look at the jeerers, who showed nothing more than planes of their faces in the torchlight. He could see teeth, cheeks, shadowy eyes. "You look nothing like him! He's tall and handsome!" The last wisecrack brought a stream of chuckles from around the gathered crowd. His bodyguard gave him another gentle push, as one nudged an ox or a cow, and Marcan kept moving. He stood on his spot and Jed took position behind him to signal he was the emperor's man. Balthasar cried out names as the other actors and their henchmen arrived on stage. "Ferran!" "Antron!" "Loreticus!" "Iskandar!" All but the last received cheers and boos, Iskandar appearing on stage with a tatty tunic under his gold to reflect his humble background. Marcan was hard put to understand who was supposed to be the hero of the story. He had always presumed he, the tragic victim, was the point of sympathy, but by the crowd's judgement everyone on stage demanded damnation.

"And then we have our ladies," continued Balthasar. "The beautiful genies of the court who might resemble certain girls from your own town." Two handsome young girls were brought on stage, one with thick, curly blonde hair and a face made up to look pinched and muscular. The other was boyish, her hair wrapped up to seem to be cut at shoulder length. "Dess," introduced Balthasar, gesturing in the direction of the blonde. Half-hearted boos and catcalls came from the crowd, followed by a deep-voiced warning from what must have been the actress's beau. "Alba," indicated Balthasar to the other. There was a choral response from the female half of the crowd, sympathetic girls and protective mothers extending their love to the lovelorn empress.

"And so, to the tale," boomed Balthasar, once more in his masterful tenor. The actors scurried around the stage to position themselves for the first act. "The emperor has awoken from a drunken sleep, to find Dess in his bed and his wife's servant knocking on his door . . ."

Marcan blundered through his lines, grateful he was out in the first act, happy the story was so fresh that no-one noticed his premature exit. Immediately he sourced wine and downed two cups without breath, then turned to watch the play unfold.

Its currency gave it weight and appeal but also left it with an open-ended fourth act which Balthasar wrapped up with a clever soliloquy. The crowd departed, and the troupe tidied up the valuables and started towards the common sleeping tent.

"You managed it," stated Balthasar as he fell in line with Marcan.

"I don't understand this drama lark yet," he returned. "Everyone on stage was such a villain. Why do people pay to come to see the play?"

Balthasar smiled and said nothing for a moment.

"Wouldn't you be rich and powerful if you could be?" he asked.

"Not if it came with that company, no," Marcan said.

"What you don't have is always more attractive than what you have. Let the villagers dream of being in the court for a night. You can dream of being a carefree actor for a summer."

Chapter 11

Marcan's dramatic skill and his nerves improved as the weeks wore on and as he settled into his lightweight role. They performed every few nights as they passed through larger villages, or after they had corralled together enough hamlets to get a buzzing audience in one place. Before every performance, Balthasar apologised to the audience for the rough edges. He explained they had changed some lines based upon intelligence from "credible sources at court" and rumours received "minutes before they arrived", and the cast was thus unprepared. This small fabrication meant even the most jaded fish wife paid close attention in case of a new nugget of information.

As the end of their season neared, Marcan's skin had settled into a dark ruddiness and the hair on his arms had bleached. A vibrant energy coursed through his body, washing out residual aches and stiffness, cleansing him of a nostalgia he wasn't aware he had been carrying. Thus was he free of age and concerns.

Balthasar took pride in Marcan's spiritual emancipation

and appeared to share his energy whenever they were together. Something of the man spoke to Marcan, encouraging him to feel a camaraderie with the elegant old actor. His humility perhaps, thought Marcan. His discretion certainly.

In each village, Balthasar went ahead to scout for any trouble that might be kindled by their political play. Army veterans settled in these rural villages, and if they had served with one of the generals there might be a reaction of loyalty or disdain. He cast one or two of the local girls to step into the roles on stage and gave them the full day to tell their friends.

On one morning, when a summer rain had woken the troupe early, Marcan asked to accompany Balthasar. Hundreds of people had seen him perform, and his confidence was growing. But like most instances of courage, it was more potent as a notion than when put to the test and Marcan fought a sickening paralysis as they entered the main market square. A strange confidence remained with him that he wasn't lost forever, that this innate but slow destiny would drag him to something unique, something glorious, something that would be played with respect on stages across the country. And yet memories came unbidden, the vision of a pack of fellow men barking and growling, chasing him to spill his blood. It was a putrid mixture of emotions which kept a permanent knot in his chest, stealing sleep and cheer. His feet slowed, sweat shone on his forehead and he began catching people's gaze to see if they still thought him the fallen emperor, Marcan the Whore. Wherever he looked the familiar face of the scandalous ruler posed proudly in profile in clay on walls.

Balthasar saw his discomfort and guided him to a tavern table. They sat, and Balthasar shielded Marcan from the passing villagers with his bulk.

"I shouldn't have come in," he stated. Balthasar observed him without response. He felt a disappointment in Balthasar. Somehow his grey hair didn't seem so elegant in the daylight, and the loss of this aura suddenly turned the rest of him into a mundane fake. Unlike Marcan, the exposure to the sun had aged Balthasar, but the complex astuteness remained in his eyes and his plump-lipped mouth. His control of everything remained, almost as if he commanded the village that surrounded him. "You look concerned," muttered Marcan without conviction. Balthasar nodded perfunctorily to the serving person over Marcan's shoulder, who had been hovering at a nearby table.

Perhaps it was his deep paranoia, perhaps his little gods were knocking on his skull, but a prickle in his back made Marcan pay attention. There was something about to happen and he became aware of the sunlight, the wooden table, the thick skin on Balthasar's hands. Then she was at the end of the table and she considered him without interest, but her eyes struck Marcan with such force that he stared. He drew in every detail he could, rifling for what made him feel like this. She was fair, her skin pale for someone in this region, her eyes the darkest blue. Bow lips moved more than they needed to as she talked to Balthasar, her collar bones bouncing slightly as she laughed with easy amusement at a quip. And then it was there, on the outside curve of her eye, that he stopped.

That shape was his, it belonged to him so thoroughly he wanted to reach out to touch the memory. She turned to look at him, and with a cold sensation, he realised it wasn't the perfection he had imagined. It was merely a beautiful imitation of something. He dropped his gaze.

"Whatever he's having," said Marcan without turning back to her.

A moment's discomfort as she nodded and looked back to Balthasar. Getting no response, moved back inside. The two men eyed each other.

"You know," said Balthasar, "you are incredibly dry."

"Balthasar, I'm not a funny man. I'm a worried man."

"If a man isn't worried about something, then he'll just go and find something to be worried about. Often as not, he'll get married so that he doesn't need to look too far in future."

Marcan remained stony faced.

"The maid would make an ideal Alba," he continued with a shrug. "We would have the best-cast performance in history in terms of lookalikes."

Marcan remained still, eyeballing the edges of his thumbs and hands. Then the waitress returned and he glanced at her and was saddened the earlier flash wasn't repeated. Balthasar started to speak, but Marcan stopped him before he could extend his invitation for the play that evening. In a simple gesture of calm uncertainty and pain, Marcan laid his hand on the old man's arm. The waitress paused after Balthasar's start to the conversation, hovered as if expecting him to speak, then placed down their clay plates and wooden mugs.

"Want to tell me anything?" asked Balthasar, his voice

low in his throat.

"No." Marcan paused, now taking in again the details of his surroundings to refresh his senses. "I don't know. My mind needs to think for a while before my mouth can talk."

Balthasar smiled. "If only more of my crew were like you," he chuckled.

But throughout the meal, Marcan's mind kept to itself, lurking at the back of his skull. It gave him no insight, jealously examining the imprint of the girl's eyes as if to find whether what they signified could be seen in a certain light. He spent time searching for something else that offered the same jolt, some other bait to bring his memory back. Everything was dull and unfamiliar.

He decided to confront his fear and to walk the streets of the town on his own, listening to the voices and noises from open windows, sliding out of the way of running children, looking for something familiar.

The town was a prosperous one. The children wore rich cloth, and the public areas were clean. The freshly buffed red buildings were square, their walls and corners making up the parameters of the streets he followed. They were all exactly the same architecture, low and elegant. The brickwork was tightly constructed, flat to his touch, and well-pruned and well-watered ornamental trees sat outside every front door in a universal fashion. Marcan tracked his walk in his mind, two streets parallel to the main rectangular plaza. In a village this size, he must be reaching the edges of the merchants' quarter. The quality of the houses demonstrated the riches gathered by these outlying pastoral regions from the capital, which had to buy its food from its country cousins.

He spun when he heard grating behind him, as if a workman was smoothing the bricks and mortar into place. This fear pervaded him, stripping him of intelligence or honour.

The scraping had been chainmail on the brick. Saguinas pressed himself flat against a warm wall, out of sight of the man he recognised immediately. Jed had been right. Here was the king of kings, drifting around a remote village in a clueless stupor. Saguinas was no politician, but he knew who would pay for this man's whereabouts.

Antron's gold would only be determined by whether he brought the emperor back alive or otherwise. Saguinas closed his eyes, breathing deliberately through his disfigured nose. He crouched, peeked around the corner again and saw his target had resumed his leisurely, complacent amble. He stared at the imperial spine, the huge expanse of unprotected flesh between his shoulder blades, and the brown nape of his neck. He itched to stick a knife in there and claim his prize.

A dog came out of the shadows, or so Saguinas thought. The shape came nearer and faster and he turned too late to catch the fist which pummelled into his blindside. A cheap blow, but one which sent him staggering. The attacker was inexperienced and didn't follow up with a stab to stop the veteran from retaliating. Saguinas righted himself, took stock of the youth before him, a blue dot painted between his brows.

"Well well well, a little zealot spy," he mocked. The boy was skinny and frightened. Two long steps, as Saguinas swallowed the ground up and took the boy by his neck in his meaty, calloused hands. He slapped the boy hard on his ear, paralysing him in pain. Saguinas pinned him up against the wall, rummaged through his clothes and then spat in his face.

"Do you want to tell me anything?"

The boy shook his head.

"Following me or him?"

"A curse on you and your bigoted family," shouted the boy. Saguinas swiftly drew his knife and slipped the blade between the boy's ribs as if he had been popping a pie.

Marcan heard the scuffling and started to move towards it, worried that someone was in danger. He loosened his neck, feeling a certain excitement in an impending fight. Small movements in the dust guided him, dry clouds floating briefly past the corner of the house. There was a groan, and Marcan sped up.

Blood pooled in the dirt on the street, spreading strangely in the scuffed tracks. Marcan looked down at the little boy, perhaps only a teenager, still alive but losing blood in a wide, deep cut. He had seen that type of wound before; something was familiar about that exact cut, as if he had been trained to do it. He looked up, around. In front of the boy, peering imperiously, was the portrait of the Emperor Marcan, forged in a colossal red clay disc.

Marcan quickly left, made a long turn around several buildings to come back to the square, and saw Balthasar. Beside him stood the waitress who had unnerved him so powerfully. She looked up as he came, and her face split into a dazzling smile which somehow made her more distant. She was no longer the person he was thinking of.

"It seems, dear Marcan, I must be your Alba tonight," she said and laughed carelessly. "I'm so excited," she continued, turning back to Balthasar. "Thank you thank you thank you." With a pious peck on his cheek, she dashed into the shadows of the bistro.

They studied each other. Balthasar quickly saw the fright in Marcan's face.

"What?" exclaimed the older man. "Forget your lines again?" He flapped a hand for Marcan to sit down.

Marcan realised that he had been holding his breath. He exhaled, making a sound with his lips.

"I'm lost, Balthasar, lost. Violence seems to follow me as tightly as my shadow and I haven't got a clue why."

"You told me that you were a naughty whore."

"Not funny. And I might have said 'bad whore' rather than 'naughty'. Isn't there someone I could turn myself over to? This country can't be so civilised without some sort of reliable administration."

"You'd be surprised," said Balthasar with a smile. "We're famous for being able to start a fight, not our ability to run a peaceful country."

"That's not good enough. That's your disappointment in life coming out."

Balthasar leant forward, his eyes rich, framed by his light hair and straight beard. "I'm not the one disappointed with my life. What can I offer you?" he purred, reading Marcan's expression incorrectly. "Nothing. Nothing at all. Be angry at me all you like but whatever sins you committed are not my fault. You aren't the type to live in ignorance for as long as you have, not without choosing to, and that self-denial is eating away your peace of mind."

"I've not chosen any of this," snarled Marcan. "To say that I am running away is a cheap assumption. Someone owes me my old life back. I'm going to be killed well before I know who I am."

"No-one owes you anything," returned Balthasar. "But you know what's missing is big. You feel it inside you, and you certainly show us every day with your sense of 'godly destiny'. It is only your lack of nerve now which stops you. You haven't asked me a single question about who I think you are."

Marcan's dark eyes pinned Balthasar now, examining his face. What did this old man know? He had presumed Balthasar wasn't bright enough to help. He was just an old warhorse.

Marcan released his fingers, spanning his palms and feeling the air enter the creases in his skin. He wondered for a moment whether the groomed man opposite him knew anything about the violence he'd witnessed.

"Maybe I don't know how to ask the questions," Marcan said. "And from you, I expected a more helpful response."

Balthasar's smile returned, and Marcan saw the sharp folds by the man's eyes, and the furrows of skin running into his beard.

"You are younger than I ever thought," Balthasar said, his smirk back. "I have had so many seasons to make me wise enough to know I can't hide from my demons. I buried them and forgot about them. Not everything needs to be solved or fixed. Some things just need to be thrown out with the rubbish."

"Turds in the stream," offered Marcan. He glanced again at the exit of the avenue. He had a choice – tell Balthasar about the dead boy or run. There was nothing helpful that could possibly come from being involved with the local militia.

Balthasar eyed him, weighing up his humour. "No, don't be so negative about these things," he replied wagging a finger. "You forget how fond I am of my bowel movements." Marcan moved his gaze to Balthasar, assessing his sudden seriousness, his judgement. Was his fear so clear on his face?

A sip of his sun-warmed wine. A small change of expression, a change of tone. "Get rid of those things in your life that don't add to your happiness. Just make sure they don't ruin your life." Another drink. "Maybe that's no solution for you, of course."

"Why not?"

Balthasar ignored him and turned to the square in front of them. The market stalls had started to pack up as the heat rose. Fish that had been brought from the nearby coast was under threat of turning bad, and amphorae of wine were becoming hot to the touch. Sweating merchants and buyers turned back home for their siestas, fresh ingredients for lunch elbow-pinched against their ribs.

"Let's find somewhere to sleep in the shade," suggested Balthasar. "There's no reason to be back early at the camp and there'll be no spare shade when we get there."

Marcan stood, letting Balthasar leave coins on the table. He looked around, saw nothing but calm and routine. No matter the logic running through his head, he couldn't escape the presumption that the dead boy around the corner was because of him.

"No, let's leave the town," he said. "I don't feel comfortable here."

"I have a sighting!" shouted Darcy, bursting through Loreticus's door. Pello, who had been reaching for the handle on the other side, fell heavily into a nearby chair.

"Grand gods, Darcy, you do know that this palace is full of spies?" asked Loreticus gently. They smiled at each other. Darcy was one of Loreticus's three trusted lieutenants who managed his once immense, complex network of informers. "Do I want to know the source or the quality?"

"Probably not, but it's most likely to be true. I've acted on this lady's information before and it's worked out well." Darcy was out of breath – as all visitors were by the time they'd reached the top of the stairs required for an interview with Loreticus. He wasn't athletic either, being of shorter than average build and predisposed to wearing fashionable rather than practical clothing.

"Then tell me," said Loreticus and unrolled a map on the desk.

"You'll need a larger one than that," said Darcy, smiling hard. "He's travelling with an acting troupe in the southern farmlands."

"A what?"

"Our emperor is hiding in plain sight as an actor."

Loreticus couldn't help but laugh. He felt all the breath leave him in a drawn, intangible sigh.

"Well, I am glad that I lived long enough to see this. How far?"

"Eight hours' hard riding," stated Darcy and indicated a cluster of small towns off the main highway. "We need to get going. If I've heard, then so have others. Expect every mercenary worth their salt to be riding down."

"But your source is on our side?"

"She's on no-one's side, so I've left her with my housekeeper. Unfortunately, she didn't realise how potent my table wine is."

"But it's breakfast," exclaimed Loreticus. "Never mind. At least you seem well enough."

"Same vintage, different cups," explained Darcy with a smirk. "I'm packed and we shall have horses outside by the time we get down. I've also sent word to Demetrian to join us."

"Need we worry about being too late?" asked Loreticus as they moved to the door.

"Always. The person who saw him is not a nice creature. Even the gangs cut him loose for being too blunt," Darcy swung the door open again. "If my friend knows, everyone will know by this evening. We need to get moving now.

"Stay here," Loreticus said to Pello as he reached the door. "Find out what you can about that necklace."

Chapter 12

That evening, the lights of the torches hovered in the darkest edges of the night. The troupe performed outside the town walls, under a moonless night. Their stage stood at the edge of a forest which breathed an anxious cold air across the cast and audience.

A bald hillock made do for the platform to their stage boards, and the townsfolk scattered themselves in patches across the small meadow, stretching out beyond the torchlight.

Ferran strode across the stage, clasping Alba in his arms. His blond hair glowed godlike, cast as a mix of gold and shadows as the torches flickered. Even in such a provincial play he was untouchable, a human from a different world, blessed by the blood of gods.

"My dear," he boomed, smacking his thick lips and turning in the direction of the audience, "how desolate you must be. You are wittolled by a worthless man, but one whom you had trusted on your father's word." The barmaid threw her face behind her hands as he continued. "How could you live with him anymore? How dare he come to the palace when he is so unworthy to represent you or the people who love him? He has debased the divine position he took so few years ago. He shall not be here anymore." With this, Ferran offered a dashing grin to the crowd, which always appeared sinister and devious in the flickering torchlight.

Antron now turned from his position in one of the unlit corners. "Let me deal with this situation," he stated, his flat cheeks sculpted in orange. A hand wrapped around the heavy sword pommel. "This insult demands a robust response." Archly, he walked near the edge of the stage, quietly and dramatically laying his hand on the shoulder of Iskandar as the latter stepped into the light.

Iskandar, the haunted general, moped over to the centre of the hillock before he saw Alba. Ever bestubbled, rings painted under his eyes to show distress and fatigue, he struggled into an upright pose, dragged himself across the stage and they draped themselves around each other in mutual anguish. Lifting his head, Iskandar winked conspiratorially at Ferran, who gave a closed-lipped grin in return.

With an inhale of breath, the crowd gasped as Marcan soundlessly stepped into the ring of light.

"My love," he began, and the cast turned to him. His hand reached out futilely from his position on one side of the stage to Alba on the other, protected by Iskandar and Ferran, who formed a wall in front of her.

"Whore!" shouted one of the extras from the shadows. It was a practised insult, which had kept the speed but lacked the urgency of its first utterance months ago. Other expletives came from the dark, encouraging the crowd to boo and whistle so loudly that any further dialogue was drowned out. Antron grabbed him with hammish violence from behind, pinning his arms to his sides and lifting him with the others' help into the shadows.

But Marcan had had more lines to say, and his mind had been struck dumb. The barmaid's eyes had been brushed by a particular angle of light and the recollection of that someone else paralysed him. That was the stupefied gaze he wore as the guards dragged him off, his stare soaking in the memory of her face, the cut of her eyes. He stopped everything, his heart resting for three long beats as he captured the moment, painting a mural inside his head.

Sitting in the crowd was a group of men wearing hoods, a fashion exported from the capital but which wasn't common in the country. There were four of them, sat quietly in a dark corner of the grassy opening. The evening air was toxic with the torch smoke when the breeze changed, and the grass was damp on their legs where they stretched over the edge of their rug.

Loreticus jumped when he heard his name called out by the troupe master. What a strange scenario: to watch yourself played on stage. The cast for the generals and the princess were close because of the gifts of busts, mosaics and etchings sent by the palace every year to the villages. But until then he had accepted that he was a name, nothing more. Was this how people imagined him?

"You look fatter on stage," whispered one of the company.

"And you, Demetrian, are better looking when played by someone else."

The play was more of a farce than an accurate report, meant to scandalise the peasantry with the implications of sex in the palace. The visitors laughed when Antron came on stage, as the ham acting caught his faked gentility well.

"Perhaps we should leave Marcan here," said Loreticus. "He seems to be enjoying himself."

"Clueless as ever."

Darcy gently nudged Loreticus's hand and gestured to a conversation at the treeline. A man who was trying to stay out of sight handed an object to a figure in stage clothing. His gestures were instructive, bullying, and he glanced around once more before slipping back out of the light of the fires.

"I'll be back in a minute," said Demetrian and quietly rose to his feet. He strode to follow the man into the shadows.

The play wrapped up, the troupe master soaking in the attention and entertainment of his audience as he delivered the epilogue. Before he left the stage, he glanced down at the city dwellers. Loreticus curled his finger discreetly at him.

"How can I help you gentlemen?" he asked as he approached. There were still a dozen families nearby, rolling up blankets and lifting their ceramic beer bottles.

"Rafael Balthasar Supramontes," croaked Loreticus. "Come sit with us a moment." He surprised himself with how easily his tradecraft came back to him, his believable country accent, his own acting skills used to con the master of the troupe. With a shy pride, he saw Darcy lurch and glance at him, unsure of where this voice had come from.

Balthasar sat meekly in front of him.

"Do you know who I am?"

"Yes, sir," replied Balthasar. The disappointment that he wasn't a better actor was rather too sharp, Loreticus realised.

"So you realise why I'm here?"

"I do."

"Well, Balthasar, we need to have a talk about why you have someone of importance prancing around like a monkey on stage. It's time for him to come home."

"Of course, sir, but this was his choice."

"Because you've informed him of the full situation, have you?" asked Loreticus. Balthasar looked down, his face hidden as the torches put silver in his hair. Loreticus reached out with his staff and lifted Balthasar's chin. "You don't think much of the three generals, do you? The drama was rather good, but the audience was a disaster. Anyway, you've had your fun. Send him to back to the capital. And dress him properly. He looks like he chose his clothes in the dark."

"Yes, sir."

Demetrian stalked into view, nudging Darcy aside and sitting next to Loreticus on the rug. Balthasar stared at the soldier's hands as he wiped them clean with the edge of the material. Blood was dark in the creases of his knuckles.

"Balthasar," he said gently. "It's been a long time, old friend."

"Yes, captain."

"I have a question for you – do you know who that was? An ugly old veteran with a face like a split pumpkin?"

"No, sir."

"Well, he was up to no good around your lot, but I managed to chase him off. Keep an eye on your men. If there's gold passing hands it must be for a sordid reason. My bets are for some violent mischief soon."

"What should I do?"

"Be his shadow for the next day," replied Demetrian. "We can't take him back with us now because the roads are thick with people looking for him."

"Give us a day to get our plans in order," said Loreticus. "If he is anything like his old self, he needs to come to us if he is to keep his pride."

Balthasar nodded.

"Tomorrow evening, send him to me," continued Demetrian. "My studio is the third building on Clearwater Street. Tell him to come there, and if for any reason he doesn't arrive, I'll have your tongue. You remember Galleus, my former sergeant. He'll be here to help you get our boy back safely."

The group stood, and the troupe master quickly followed. He was, Loreticus noted, still a man with his military gait despite the dramatic beard and hair. He hoped that his judgement of Balthasar was true and that Marcan remained safe for the next day.

"And the man in the woods?" asked Balthasar. "It could cause trouble."

"I don't know," said Demetrian. "He's somewhere out there. I'll have to take my horse to follow him."

He turned, following Darcy and Loreticus to the horses. "My lord," he said, "I'm going after that man. I think that I recognised him. My guess is that he lives in the local village, so I'll be back tomorrow with any luck."

Loreticus nodded and turned his horse away, back in the direction of the main road to the capital.

Chapter 13

That night he dreamed of the girl, but he didn't see her eyes. There was no colour in the dream, and he was standing away from her, to watch her as they looked out from a high-crested hill. She stood, younger in form and posture, her hair longer and pulled back in a simple ponytail in the same way as the barmaid. She was watching a heavy grey rain cloud as it spread across the valleys in front of her, the diagonal shafts of rain fluffing the underside. The breeze that came before a rainstorm was already with them, prickling his skin with its warmth and moisture. It playfully pulled at her hair, drawing her ponytail to one side and making the hair against her skull into a lopsided shape as it pressed and pulled. He knew that when the rain came and the winds strengthened she would stay. In this dream, she didn't turn around nor did she consider him in case she missed the majestic storm. He held this sensation of love and cold skin, of respect and solitude. When he awoke to the night's last stars in a turquoise pre-dawn, he felt less of a man because now he knew something of his loss.

"There was a murder here yesterday," stated Balthasar as they packed in a hurry. "Obviously, we're going to get blamed. We always do."

"Are we suspects?" asked Marcan. Any interaction with the militia was troubling. If he was a whore, he could easily be considered as a thief or a murderer. Finding out in front of a hanging magistrate was not the best option.

"Want to take the chance they'd give us preferential treatment when there's blood on their well-polished cobblestones?"

Balthasar barked instructions of urgency to his troupe, who glanced at him, then Marcan. Marcan watched him as he approached, opened his mouth to say something and then thought better of it. He turned back and looked for someone else to shout at.

"Do you think that I am involved in this?"

"No, of course not," stated Balthasar without any conviction. "This is a mugging gone wrong. Whatever it is, best we move on and let the lynch mob beat up the other tourists."

Balthasar was getting more anxious by the minute, and yet somehow his focused gaze took in everything but Marcan. He counted the bags and the horses and watched his team move. He shook his head or gestured with his chin when necessary. All the while though, Balthasar kept his shoulder turned away from Marcan ever so slightly, enough to say he acknowledged his presence but wished he wasn't there.

Marcan turned his attention from the rush in front of them to consider Balthasar's expression. The man could wear his extravagant ashen beard and the great volume of hair with such panache because of his dark, animated eyes. They told the world everything about the man behind them and Marcan was beginning to understand their language. Balthasar was holding on to a lie about Marcan which had been obvious since the beginning. That Marcan had left it with Balthasar was his own choice, but now he saw it was a folly. His recuperation was over. He was the stronger man now and that was the secret Balthasar had wanted to hide. He had no need to protect Marcan anymore.

"Tell me," he asked Balthasar once the entourage had packed their bags and their inertia, "what is your obsession with using travellers' huts to crap in?"

Balthasar glanced at him but kept walking. "Well, dear Marcan, I'm one of those people who enjoy a fresh movement but hate the result," he replied. "A stream purifies everything about the practice. It stops me being an animal. These guys . . ." he gestured with a flick of his hand in the direction of the three rough cast members in front of them, "act the part of the generals every night and then go to drop their trousers in the woods the next morning. I doubt any of those great men deign to poop. Fight like a god and then strain like a dog? I think not."

Marcan stared past them, watching the dirt on the road. There wasn't the imprint of a single footstep, but rather a hundred thousand of them blurred into a flat breadth.

"Do you know more about me than you're telling me?" he asked.

"Bit of a change of subject," remarked Balthasar.

"I know more about these people than I do about myself," stated Marcan, gesturing with his arm. "And not just because I listen, but because they all talk easily about themselves. You observe everyone and I know you've spent time thinking about who I am. You never bring it up, never offer an opinion or a solution. Never give me direction."

"Because everyone in this world would offer a king's ransom to spend a season without guilt or regret. You are in the middle of a marvellous luxury if you were wise enough to enjoy it. Maybe I'm letting you have that little extra time."

Balthasar's naturally dominant personality was tempered when he spoke to Marcan, and this played to Marcan's paranoia.

Even Balthasar now seemed unconvinced himself. He looked swiftly around, spying a roadside hut as if he hadn't noticed it before.

"I'll be back in a while," he said. The troupe came to a gradual rest behind them as packs were dropped and fires lit. Marcan raised his chin and turned to look for a cup of warm wine and honey. The morning banter rarely changed unless there had been a performance day before. It was the usual rehash of plans, lost loves, and the other myths and legends of the small community. Normally he listened in, as if it were a familiar song with its rhythms and verses, but today he sat counting moments as he played with the smell of the drink.

The worm of suspicion had crawled into him and now he needed to understand more. Balthasar was a poor liar and a poor friend not to be offering what he needed. Perhaps it was time that he made this man less of a friend and more of someone of use.

Marcan had a destiny and Balthasar was smothering it.

The door swung open silently, the sudden sunlight shocking Balthasar. Marcan entered, shadows darkening his brows. He sat with a heavy refinement on the bench by the side of the hut, resting his sandaled feet in the pepperings of light, before he looked up. Balthasar sat on his folding crap chair, the water chattering happily underneath.

"Hi," said Balthasar. "Something on your mind?"

Marcan was silent. He focussed on his breathing.

"Just here for the company? I might offer better conversation in a while."

Balthasar scrutinised the man, unsettled more by the change in his demeanour than by his looming presence. Marcan was a towering man, not necessarily much taller than the average, but his bearing was like a wall of air around him which demanded respect and concern. Balthasar hesitated in his thoughts.

"What do you want?" he asked again, more directly. A moment's silence, then Marcan's eyes changed. It was a new face, thought Balthasar, as if his old soul had come to rest at last. The realisation made his morning ritual a distant memory. Unexpectedly his foot was dancing without consent. He got angry at this candid unease, of the loss of control Marcan had enforced without a word.

"Damn!" growled Balthasar. "Speak, you idiot. Do you think I can read minds?"

Marcan stood with dramatic speed, snapping crisply to attention. He moved elegantly nearer to the squatting figure and crouched down in front of him.

"Who do you think I am?" he asked calmly. "I already know, but you need to say."

Balthasar couldn't answer. Thousands of small conversations and responses ran through his head.

"Who," repeated Marcan, "do you think I am?"

"You are the missing emperor, you fool," whispered Balthasar angrily. "Marcan of the New Kingdom. The leader of the armies, the husband of Alba, the son-in-law of the late Augustus himself."

Marcan felt a coolness run through his veins, watching Balthasar squirm like a rodent before a predator. Gone were the laughter lines, the boyish tics, the charming readiness to laugh. "I wanted to keep you safe whilst you regained your sanity," Balthasar explained to the stranger. "If you weren't ready, why would I expose you to a hundred assassins as an innocent man?"

"You kept me like a prize animal in the zoo," replied Marcan, his voice quiet and determined. "You kept me at your pleasure."

Balthasar's body spasmed at the prospect of this judgement. He was immediately shrunken, stress thumping inside his head.

"Do the other men know?" Macan asked.

"Everyone sees it every time we walk past an imperial clay portrait. No-one believes it as far as I am aware. It's too bizarre."

Silence. Marcan examined Balthasar, catching the lines and the silver hair, the fear and the stress.

"Why should you know and they not?"

"Because I had a visit from my old boss at the last performance. He brought Loreticus the Intelligencer," stated

Balthasar.

Another moment of silence. Then in his newly adopted swiftness, Marcan stood again.

"If Loreticus believes in you, you could be the most powerful man in the world," said Balthasar. "Whether you are Marcan or not."

Marcan walked to the door, and before he slipped out, he said, "Find me later to prepare for my return to the capital."

Balthasar told Jed and Samwer to sit in front of him. They were away from The Psittacis, hidden in the edge of the wood. Everyone else was eating or sleeping during the lunch rest. The birds were singing, noisily, their calls echoing between the trees. The clearing smelled of ancient mulch and moss, the duff kicking up fungal scents as they walked.

"It's off," said Balthasar, stress squeezing his voice.

"No," said Samwer, looking over to Jed.

"Yes," replied Balthasar. "What you don't know is that the real Demetrian and Loreticus came to watch our last performance. They want their prince back."

"So what? He's not even the real Marcan," said Jed. "But if Loreticus says he is, then there's gold in it. Let's tell Saguinas that we want more. We've got proof now."

"Jed, you're starting a game I don't want to play. These are not the men you tease," warned Balthasar. He sucked the hair of his beard. It wasn't a pleasant taste, carrying sweat, old food and wine.

"I have no intention of teasing them. We give a figure and then take what we are offered."

"It's not like that. They have me responsible for his return."

"Then we do it, and you protest your innocence."

"I can't do that," said Balthasar, putting his face in his hands. "You don't know these people. They scare me. If you anger Loreticus, you vanish from the street or you die in your sleep. I've seen Demetrian slaughter five men on his own. We are actors. Don't confuse us with the real generals."

"You were a veteran," said Samwer.

"Still am, son," replied Balthasar. "That makes me wise, not invincible." He leant forward, catching the gaze of both of them. "It's off. If they even find out that we were plotting to do this, we're dead. If we don't deliver him untouched, we're dead. If we don't protect him from Saguinas, we're dead. Do you see how this is going?"

They both nodded.

"At least he has brought us a profitable summer," sighed Balthasar. "Count the small blessings."

The two men nodded and grumbled unconvincingly as they wandered back towards the fires. Balthasar watched them. For good actors, they were terrible liars and he knew that they had a contingency plan.

He looked over at the satchel he carried close everywhere. In that bag was a written promise from the imperial spymaster, a promise which matured on the safe delivery of Marcan. That piece of paper would change Balthasar's life, and make him a moneyed man. He was damned if those two idiots would take a share. He had spent the summer training that boy to act, talk and behave like the emperor.

Balthasar was the best that money could buy. Jed and Samwer would have to find their own riches.

Chapter 14

Loreticus watched the door in the massive red wall. He sat, drinking the ale from the street stall, enjoying the bouncing shadows of leaves twenty feet in the air. The walls were elegant, distant with their enormity, robust and ancient.

The culture of the market was split in two by the corda barrelling through the middle of it. On one side, everyone was friends, with laughter and conversations rife. Over the other side, each person wore their dark hood up in the traditional style, covering their face, demonstrating the right to privacy. Hardly a word was spoken, with each interaction engaged through economical gestures of merchandise or offered coins.

The traffic on the corda was the stream of chaos. Cart drivers were yelling at anyone they could find to swear at, often gesticulating passionately but not even looking at the subject of their insults.

As a merchant or a buyer crossed the corda from the darker side and was subjected to the ignominy of the drivers' tongues, he quickly became animated and joined the cheerful whole.

A rigid figure sat down at his table and Loreticus gently settled his drink on the wooden surface. He looked carefully at the newcomer, feeling himself prepare for a violent attack. Blood was being spilled on the streets now, as if the capital was suffering referred pain from the court. Loreticus had wondered how long it would take for his threat to outweigh his value to Antron. His reputation had always been his currency; now it was a target on his back as Marcan's loyalists whispered his name as their saviour.

But the figure drew his hood back, revealing the dry face of Selban, warped with age and whatever disease sat on his bones. Whenever Loreticus saw that face, there was a certain sympathy. An intelligent man cursed by a broken body. It was Selban's own flaw however that had let him stain his morals.

"Hello, Loreticus."

"Selban." Loreticus gestured to the maid, who brought out another cup.

"Rain on the horizon," Selban muttered with his gaze fixed on the mountains, which sat in the frame of the long straight street. Loreticus looked down, between the tottering buildings to the plum clouds breaking over grey mountains.

"Grim, indeed," he said. He wished he had his pipe. On occasions like these, he felt he was in for a long wait until Selban was ready to talk. "Did you find me easily enough?"

"Rather, seeing as you didn't tell me where you'd be," replied Selban with a yellow smile.

"No, there wasn't an invitation, was there?" He gave

up his struggle and gestured for a hawker with a basket to come over with a pipe and tobacco. He prepared it in silence and took a refreshing first draw. "Where's Darcy?"

"Off tickling someone's testicles, I should imagine. Offering a favour now for one 'to be cashed in the future'." He mimicked Darcy's mock-aristocratic tones. For a terrible moment, Loreticus thought he might cup his hands and stick out his tongue in demonstration, but Selban was simply removing something from his line of sight.

A slightly uncomfortable breeze came from the clouds, down the mountains and along the road to their table.

"What exactly might I do for you, dear Selban?"

Selban nodded at the high red wall. "I've been gathering information on your boy as well," he said. "We need to talk."

Between their table and the red walls, dozens of people crossed every moment. Heavily armoured palace soldiers stood lazily nearby, their stance relaxed but their eyes vigilant under the polished brass of their helmets. They used to be Demetrian's men. Now, in their new silver and dark-red doublets, they were as strange and threatening as an invading army.

"Have you met with the generals yet?" asked Loreticus.

"Yes. You?"

"Just. Nothing new there," he stated. "I'm expecting a blade between the ribs from them in the not too distant future. There's no match at all."

"No, although Iskandar isn't his normal sunny self, even considering his wife's holiday." Selban gestured to the maid with his empty cup. "I had my morning meal with Darcy earlier and asked him whether he had been summoned by the Big Noses. He said he hadn't."

"It's coming, I'm sure. They'll do the rounds of the loyalists and the troublemakers," said Loreticus.

"Well, the thing is, my dear spymaster, that the generals let me know they had already met our third wheel." They eyed each other, Loreticus concerned and Selban smug. "I thought he might mean he hadn't committed to anything with them, or he hadn't had a decent conversation with them, yah-de-yah. But as the conversation went on, I became more sceptical of his story."

"Do you trust him?" enquired Loreticus.

"Generally, or with the generals?" Selban folded his arms. "Honestly, I fear he is as loyal as the wind blows. If we find Marcan, there is a fair chance he trades him in for security with Antron's mob. I don't think our Darcy has the stomach for a fist fight."

"I give Darcy credit. He's made a clever line out of that business that most of us find unprofitable – the art of living very well."

"And my thought is that he wouldn't like to risk that."

You think he's turned?" asked Loreticus slowly.

"The generals aren't smart enough to engage in bluffs and double-play. They get their answers and stab you if you give the wrong one. So yes, I think our little friend has turned."

"Hmmm," Loreticus mused and sent javelins of smoke through his nostrils. "I don't blame him. Even my own guard seems to be nervous at the generals' brazen tactics. Three of Marcan's bankers have been slaughtered and their estates taken, all using the authority of the throne. Every person who supported the missing emperor, or at least doesn't declare newly found loyalty to the generals, is prey. No, it's certainly not their cunning we should worry about. Darcy's smarter than all three put together, so for them it truly was a coup. Selban, you really do complicate my life. Ever the carrier of bad news and disappointment."

"Well," replied Selban, "you should have seen my mother when she first saw my ugly face."

"What of the matter of the necklace?" asked Loreticus. "Have you and Pello found anything out?"

"More concrete news there. This wasn't the only piece to go missing. Apparently, the man was carrying a box of Iskandar's private coins somewhere when he was bashed and cut. The murderers made off with the box," said Selban.

"And went on to murder another ten people?"

"Doesn't make sense, does it? Separate attacks."

"No, the same hand certainly," stated Loreticus. "Zealot hit squads on a random raid? Barbarians? It really doesn't click."

"Let's presume that this was the first attack in a planned series," said Selban, levelling his finger at his colleague. This was the genius of Selban, the ability to find the raw red thread which ran through random events. Loreticus watched him with an eager anticipation. "What does the box of gold then become?"

"Payment for the night's work." Loreticus's head started swimming. The chatter and ruckus from the street buried a lot of his thoughts; Selban was waiting to start again. Loreticus focused on the taste of his apple smoke to bring him back.

"Indeed. The box transfer was a setup. Only Iskandar could order the transfer of such a collection of his valuables." Selban stuck his finger in the air. "Or perhaps his wife's valuables."

"Unless a thief took it out past the guards. But that's near impossible and it doesn't make sense. Why rob a general when you could burgle a merchant? So, no zealots, no pending invasion," concluded Loreticus, blowing his smoke into a thin line. He looked up at the thunder clouds over the mountains. "It can't be. This must have been planned from within. Maybe I was wrong and the generals have been bluffing me with their gormlessness all along."

"If Iskandar knew what was coming and was moving his wife's jewellery out of the house, why have it stolen?"

Loreticus shrugged. The question was valid.

"Because he's broke," he said. "He's got no cash."

"Indeed," agreed Selban. "And rather his wife's valuables than his own. My guess is that he didn't know that any had the family mark on it. He didn't organise this on his own though. Antron needed to have pulled them all together."

"What a fool Iskandar is to get into bed with those two."

"Loreticus, my friend, you were born rich and connected. You have lived a life of abstracts. Your ability to persuade is unsurpassed, your charm is legendary and you've used it to convince people to put their necks on the line time after time. You are a hypocrite if you're saying that you don't understand how people can be persuaded against their better judgement."

"But Iskandar is a smart man, not some moneylender we need to squeeze," stated Loreticus. His pipe had turned cold. He put it down.

"Yes, he is a smart man, and you are too. But there are people in this world you will never understand because you have soft hands and a lack of compromise."

Loreticus sat for a while after Selban had disappeared, staring at the tall red walls and considering the damage that had just been confirmed. Of the possibilities for the disappearance of Marcan, this was the worst because it was the most imminent. It also showed preparation and determination by the very men he wanted least as his enemies, and those who already treated him as a threat.

With a crushing nausea, he realised that the palace guards who were constantly following him weren't an empty threat from bullies. They truly were waiting for an opportunity to butcher him in the dirt. Loreticus closed his eyes and rested them in his palms. What an arrogant idiot he was, believing his own reputation at the risk of his life.

He stood and flicked his hood up in the shade outside the bar as he waited for his moment. He had seen some familiar faces enter through Alba's private entrance and he was waiting for them to leave; when the two men exited, Loreticus caught the chin of Demetrian poking out from under his hood.

He walked to the door a few moments after they had gone and the soldier once again knocked. He was keenly aware of how close they stood to each other, and he glanced down surreptitiously at the hand which sat on the great hexagonal pommel of the sword hilt.

The door opened and he bolted through, the skin between his shoulder blades prickling with tenderness, down the columned corridor, spinning right in the direction of Alba's private chambers.

She took a double look when he burst in, first surprise, then guilt.

"Loreticus," she said, a fragility carrying in her throat.

"Alba, my darling." He drifted over and kissed her on both cheeks, foregoing the usual hug as she instinctively drew her torso into a clench. He glanced down to see what she was looking at–a map of the southern towns and villages with a coin placed on a certain spot. "Planning to travel?"

"Planning to tell me that you saw Marcan?" she snapped. He reached down and moved the coin away from the village name, the location at which he and Demetrian had seen the troupe perform.

"Yes, I was when I eventually saw him."

"I don't understand what you're talking about."

"The actor we saw was not Marcan," stated Loreticus. "He was a perfect lookalike but a terrible actor and no emperor. He looked like a penniless artist who lives by shagging old widows."

"That morality he shares with the emperor must come with that certain face then," Alba muttered.

"I thought the same." Loreticus stared at her. "We have a chance, Alba, to rebuild the throne and to do it better than anyone else. You and I can make this actor the real thing. You and I will run this empire until there is a real heir to the throne."

"Don't talk to me about children," she muttered. "You expect me to live with an absolute stranger as my husband? You've made him sound a fool and a braggart."

"Count your options and then get angry at me," scoffed Loreticus. Everyone seemed intent on setting fire to his plans. Perhaps he should simply let them burn. "You summoned Demetrian without asking me first. What's going on, princess?"

Alba walked away from him so that the table was between them.

"Why do these people promise one thing whilst intent on doing something completely different?"

"Who?"

"Cousin Ferran, the others."

"Oh, tradition mainly."

"Then why is he called 'Antron the Brave'?" she asked, exasperated.

"Because he's brave." Loreticus shrugged dramatically. "Don't be so naive to imagine that means that he's honest as well." He was annoyed about her questioning his man; people complicating his plans irritated him. He was setting something in motion and he had no intention of repeating hard work because someone felt left out. "So, what did Demetrian say?"

"That he met one of Antron's thugs on the road back."

"Saguinas?"

"Maybe. Apparently, he's 'no longer a concern'. But before he stopped being a concern, he told Demetrian that Antron had put a generous bounty on Marcan's head."

"Really?" Loreticus sat back in a soft chair by the wall and folded his arms. He stared at the window opposite, lips pursed.

"So?" asked Alba after a moment. Loreticus raised his eyebrows and stuck his chin out at her. He and Alba had a decades-long tradition of nagging and being nagged for her one-word questions. "So, what do we do?"

"We bring back Marcan," Loreticus said with a half-smile, standing again and coming near her.

"Regardless of whether he's the original Marcan or not?"

He looked down at the map once more, tapping his finger.

"I need to talk to Demetrian," he replied. "First, I need to confess something to you. We think that we know the culprits behind this grand scheme."

"Who?"

"Let's go for a walk in your garden. This palace has perforated walls and you never know who's behind them."

Loreticus took Alba's elbow, guiding her through her entrance hall and out in to the thick foliage of her outdoor reception.

Alba had hidden from Loreticus for almost the entire summer, embarrassed and uncomfortable. Now she let him set the scene. She was angry, bothered that he had bought her connivance for his grand plan, but was now deserting her to his own adventures. She sat with a thump on a marble bench between the leaves. If Loreticus did not share what he knew now, Alba could easily step in to learn what she needed. Loreticus's expression showed that he understood that. She thought that he had always been rather studied in his mannerisms, and she waited as he returned his gaze with the appropriate mood created.

"A messy business," he said.

"Not a sordid one?"

"No," he said. He walked up to her low stone bench, which sat in the warm breeze, which circulated in her private garden. Lifting her hand from the arm, he encouraged her to stand and laid her fingers on his forearm as they walked into the sunlight. Whenever he spoke, he tended to lean his head to her as he had done when she was twelve and she needed the obvious intimacy. "Staged, I believe. I don't know how but I'll find out."

"Who?"

"Who do you think, princess?"

The warmth of the sun radiated on their ankles and calves from the sandstone path. Broad leaves either side of them mixed the air like blades.

"Why?"

"Because they could," he said in a resigned voice. "I think–and this is without proper consideration or evidence–I think he had isolated himself from you, from me, from Demetrian, and from his favourite informer, my little Darcy. He was tired, lax and running in circles." He stopped, picked the leaf from a small plant and popped it in his mouth. "Life is so much clearer when you're chasing things. You have a goal and therefore an advantage over those who must manage everything. I'm not sure how Iskandar is involved, or whether he employed any of his brains in this tavern farce, but the rest bears the typical stamp of Antron."

"Loreticus, there are some things I can do which you can't."

"That I know, my lady, but perhaps you might give me an indication of what you mean."

"I'll ask one of them quite directly."

"Oh, well I could do that," considered Loreticus.

"No, you couldn't. Firstly, it's not in you. It's not in the rules of your game. Secondly, they are quite comfortable killing you. I'm a different target however."

"Very true. So who is your victim?"

"The weakest, of course."

Alba knew she would draw a punishment down on the generals and the jezebel who sabotaged her husband, but first she needed to know everything, every small grimy detail.

So, she called Iskandar to an audience. The great general stood awkwardly upon arrival, caught somewhere between reverence for royalty and self-confident pride. As a military man, he was unmatched with his striking physique and fighting ability. But it was clear when he had joined the court that he might be the best of the soldiers but nowhere near the best of the courtiers. His influence had been assumed by Antron, often against Marcan.

Thus, the veteran general stood, unsure of whether Alba was enemy or neutral, whether her blood and her marriage gave her authority or a handicap. But like most new men he was more eager to obey than to be cast out as a country fool.

"Do you have anything to tell me about the scandal?" asked Alba directly. She left him standing as she poised on a giant ceremonial chair.

"I don't understand, your highness," he retorted. "I am at as great a loss as yourself."

"I do doubt that," snapped Alba. Iskandar's face registered surprise at her anger. "General, I have extended periods of being a princess but it isn't a permanent affliction. Be aware that I won't put up with any of your politickings."

"Yes, my lady."

"So, I'll ask you again. Were you involved in that spectacle with your wife?"

"I didn't know anything about her activities," he responded, gaze down. He was a better general than liar.

"So, this was all those two?"

"I must presume so, my lady."

"And where is he now?"

"We don't know, my lady."

"You don't know? Did you lose the emperor so quickly?" Silence. "I assure you, general, if my husband is hurt in any way my father's temper will come out in me. I am not without influence and you should remember that. I shall wield that authority like an axe should I find myself a widow."

Iskandar stood straight, not pride but challenge in his gaze.

"I exiled your wife and I control her visits. She is now kept under guard by the imperial cohort in one of my family's forts. She'll not be back soon, but then I should imagine that is a blessing for you. She did, after all, break your heart."

No response. Alba watched for a moment, reading his eyes as they stared at something behind her.

"Don't think that you can rescue her. After all, I am still the empress and you remain my obedient general."

His eyes moved to connect with her own.

"Did the generals tell you otherwise? That she would be protected afterwards? I'm afraid, my dear Iskandar, that you seem to have some tuning required in your little choir. The trouble with military types is that you think only of the battle and not the day afterwards. You should have planned a cleverer exit for her than into the middle of my guards." She folded her slender arms, sharp elbows protruding. "She will remain safe as long as he is. When he is back, you can find out your emperor's decision yourself."

There was an impatience, an anger in Iskandar, and Alba enjoyed watching him for a moment. This was her empire, her blood in the red of this palace. Perhaps it was time that Loreticus, Marcan and the generals understood that. She sent him away to his urgent matters.

Chapter 15

"So, the actor isn't Marcan?" asked Darcy later that afternoon. The sun was an hour away from setting and families were retreating in to their homes to cook and rest.

"No," said Demetrian, cutting something in front of him on the counter in his kitchen.

"Yes, he is Marcan," retorted Loreticus, eying the veteran. "But he's changed quite a lot after a summer on the road. He's skinnier and scruffier."

"Why do you do women's work?" Darcy enquired.

"You're questioning my manliness?" said Demetrian, turning to Darcy with the knife in his hand.

"No, no, not at all."

"When did you find out about the actor?" croaked Selban. He sat in the darkness of the corner of Demetrian's table. A cloud of sweet pipe smoke hovered in a halo over his head. It spread, drifting in to the late sunbeams on the far side of the room.

"Who? Me?" responded Darcy. "Less than an hour before you did. I was having breakfast with one of my lovely informants. Why?"

"What he's asking you, Darcy, is whether you told Antron or Ferran about Marcan's location," said Loreticus from his seat. He spoke gently, angling to diffuse the long-brewing spat between his agents. Loreticus punched the tobacco into his pipe bowl, and watched in irritation as Darcy and Selban swapped looks of dislike.

"Of course not. Isn't it more likely that you have a spy in your offices?" asked Darcy of Loreticus.

"Graceful gods, no," replied the tall man. "Pello doesn't have the wit and no-one else was there. It was just us lot." He paused. "Sorry, Pello, I didn't mean to be rude."

Pello smiled.

Demetrian lifted a plate of pale meats over to the smoking skillet by the window and laid slabs on to the burning metal. Quickly a smell of frying gammon went to battle with the pipe smoke.

"I don't know how you two can smoke those pipes in this heat," said Demetrian. "It's cloying. But to answer the question you're all dancing around, Saguinas obviously got paid twice."

"And that's not the only question," stated Loreticus. "Saguinas said that it was only Antron who offered the bounty?"

"Yes."

"Then I wonder whether that was because neither of the other two were in the room or because they didn't know about it. I'll have to twist handles and push doors to find out. This party was not built to last."

Darcy stood up and moved next to Demetrian. He looked in the pan and pointed.

"That one, please."

Demetrian eyeballed him. The shorter man looked back.

"I like the edges crispy, please," said Darcy.

"Pello, I need your help with something . . . personal. Would you mind straying slightly from your usual tasks?"

"Of course not, Loreticus. Is it about Alba or Dess?"

"Neither, of course," snapped Loreticus and peered at Pello from under his eyebrows, not in reproach but in concern at how much he, the spymaster, was letting slip. He must be tired because he thought he had always been scrupulous with his words.

He didn't continue the conversation, but instead led Pello at pace towards the broad avenue where the grander residences stood. Behind, his cohort of guards creaked and rustled in their leather armour, the noise of their impending approach parting the crowd in front of them.

The buildings were the oldest in the capital, some as old as the palace itself. The walls were smooth, the roofs shallow peaks, and everything about their architecture implied years of basking in the golden sun. The crowd in front were also different to the usual citizens. They were taller, healthier, gentler in their gestures. They didn't turn to see who the guards were escorting because here everyone had protection.

Loreticus led them to one large building, set back slightly from its neighbours, well appointed and well maintained. It was painted in a dark apricot hue, the borders to the windows and its first-floor balconies in white. Something of the house radiated a spiritual warmth, a rich homeliness contained but not brazen. As Loreticus went to the servants' entrance along the side of the building, he saw Pello's confusion.

"Insightful in some things and surprised by others, eh?" He chuckled. "You really are my piecemeal spy."

Two guards went in, checking the rooms for unwanted visitors, then came out and fell in line with their colleagues. Loreticus and Pello entered.

The kitchen was still dark and they walked slowly as their eyes became accustomed to the shadows. Loreticus split a blind open a small amount to let in a beam of light, enough now to illuminate the whole room.

He sat at the long, smooth table and started prodding his pipe bowl. Pello stood for a moment watching, then pulled out a chair and sat.

"Pello, what do you want to ask me?"

"I don't think that I have any burning questions," said the boy.

"You do. What do you not understand?"

Loreticus watched as Pello traced the grain of the wood with his fingers.

"The generals killed the emperor?"

"The generals ordered Marcan to be drugged, but they didn't anticipate that they would kill him. The fools hired incompetents, and between them they assassinated our emperor. I have seen the body of Marcan with my own eyes," replied Loreticus.

"Why are they still looking for him then?"

"Why do you think?" returned Loreticus.

"Because they don't know that he's dead?"

"That's right. The poison they gave him to sleep wasn't good. He didn't last until midday. He managed to escape from Antron's supervision and get word to me. By the time I arrived, he was already dead." Loreticus looked up to see the effect that this was having on the boy. "Can you imagine the bloodshed if it was known that one, or all three, of the generals had poisoned the anointed emperor? The civil war we struggled through with the zealots would be nothing in comparison to the great armies fighting each other. The empire would have committed swift, brutal suicide within a season and history would remember us forever as fools."

Pello's face was pale, completely without expression as he worked through the logic.

"If he died, how did the physician not recognise him?" Pello enquired.

"I made sure that he wouldn't be recognisable," responded Loreticus, and for a moment he watched his hands on his knees. "No-one else could know."

"Balthasar?" he asked. Loreticus nodded. "Alba?" Loreticus nodded again. "Demetrian?"

Loreticus didn't respond at first, but puffed on his pipe.

"This isn't something to discuss with Demetrian. He is a loyal man, as he must be, and his logic works in different ways to mine."

"But he is at fault as well," stated Pello. "He let the emperor get taken."

"His guards were murdered, which was something no-one could foresee," said Loreticus slowly. Even though it hadn't been his hand which had cut their throats, he felt a deep guilt at putting them in harm's way.

"Did you give them leave that night?"

"Not directly."

"So you knew of the plot against Marcan?" It was the first time Loreticus had heard judgement in Pello's voice, and it was the first time for a long time that he accepted that he needed judging.

"I am the imperial spymaster, Pello. I know almost everything of importance in this barren, immature little country of ours. Yes, I had heard. Yes, I share the blame. But no, I am not like them."

He paced over to the kitchen door, which led to a shadowy hall.

"Have you an idea of where we are, Pello?"

"Your old house," replied the boy. "Mother brought me here on my first trip to the capital."

Loreticus nodded at the memory.

"I come here to think. When your logic forces you to do things that go against the very fabric of your person, it is easy to doubt yourself. Here I can sit and remember that an intelligent person, someone far wiser than me, believed in me."

"Aunt Dhalia?"

"She loved this kitchen. She loved the subtlety of cooking, and seeing how her creations captivated her guests. Dhalia rarely told them that she had been involved; simply seeing them happy and at peace was enough." He smiled as a thought matured, his old smile which spread and closed his eyes. "The spymaster and the secret cook. Rather ironic, don't you think?"

Chapter 16

There was no sense of satisfaction at hearing his suspicion confirmed. He felt a fool, unworthy of even his own skin, and he couldn't be around these people who had laughed with him over the summer. He shrank into himself, his thoughts sprinting into each other as he tried to make sense of everything. Balthasar had told him to go back the next day, and they would arrange the details as the troupe set off after breakfast. Demetrian's man would come back to find him.

Marcan lay under a wool blanket and a waxed cloth, his sleeping mat flat against the grass of the field, feeling like a toy passed from one child to the next. A deep impatience churned his thoughts, an annoyance at these flawed men who seemed intent on handicapping his destiny. But then he considered that maybe it was his cowardice that gave them that influence, maybe he needed to deserve his destiny. It seemed now that he had run out of time. This week or next he would pack his bags and find his way on his own, either further south or up to the capital. Whichever way would shed him of Balthasar and his grubby network. Long gone was the day when he would open the door to a stranger because a coin toss told him so. Now he would only act when he had one option, and then it was hesitantly.

With that resolved in its own involuntary way, a sense of longing urged him to capture these final moments of freedom and he stared at the stars.

A scuffling stabbed at his attention and his ears strained to grasp the detail. He could feel his breath wheezing and his heart tumbling inside his ribs. The rest of the troupe slept under a communal tarpaulin twenty feet away, out of earshot and out of thought.

Again, something like the drag of feet on the grass. Marcan reached for the stick which he used for walking, clutching it as if he had drawn it from a scabbard. Once more the noise, and this time with purpose. His ears were aching with concentration, and reactively he leapt up, stick poised.

A whistle, which he realised too late was something thin whipping past his face. He lashed out in the direction of the attacker's legs, made contact and provoked a yelp. Rapidly he snapped his arm in short arcs, bashing the attacker's ankle and knee.

"Ow damn, ow bollocks."

Marcan's excited blood gave him a sharper vision in the dark and he started to make out an uncertain silhouette. He saw the head and reflex turned his hand, his own knee leading the swing and drawing the torsion of his body into a thunderous blow. Bones cracked and flesh split. The attacker sat backwards.

"Owwwwwwww daaaaaaaaaaamn," he whined resignedly.

A torch was lit and Balthasar stormed over. The hand that held the stem of the light was shiny with blood. He swept light over Marcan, looking for puncture marks, then turned to the sitting figure.

"What the hell did you think, Jed?" he shouted incredulously. "That you were going to get rich from a dead man in a field? You're both damned idiots." He kicked the man in the shoulder with the heel of his boot, flattening him against the ground. "This is his blood. Samwer's blood. He's lying over there by the tarpaulin and I have no idea whether he's alive or dead. But he's certainly moving less than you."

Balthasar sucked in a gallon of air through his rasping nostrils, desperately trying to calm himself. Marcan could see the others standing just out of torchlight, their shapes smudged.

"What do you want to do?" asked Balthasar.

"What can we do?" returned Marcan. "Get Demetrian's man. Who knows who these two have told already."

"No-one," said Jed pitifully. "We've told no-one. We thought they'd take the reward. When we talked–"

"Shut up, you inbred peasant dog cocker," Balthasar growled.

"What do you suggest?"

"I'll work something out. I can't find Galleus," grumbled Balthasar. "Off to bed, the lot of you!" The spectators turned silently and quickly, somehow relieved of their morbid duty to watch.

"Wasn't he supposed to be my shadow?"

Balthasar kept his eyes on Jed but spoke to Marcan. "My instinct is that your bodyguard is in a stream with a knife in his guts. You're leaving tomorrow morning. You're going to see the real-life Demetrian rather than this pig sucker who acts in his name."

Again, dictated to, but the panic on Balthasar's face gave Marcan a level of satisfaction. This was destiny, not the troupe master's ploy. Marcan was finding his path now.

"Do you need this man?" asked Marcan, an edge leading his voice. Balthasar shook his head, never breaking Jed's startled gaze.

A moment passed, then Marcan swung the stick so fast it left only a loop on the memory of the eyes. A hollow *crock* as the end struck Jed's forehead and dropped him to the ground.

"Leave me with him," said Marcan. "I need to make sure."

When dawn broke, Marcan sat by the edge of the camp, watching the sun's early presence crawl across the damp plateau. A broad figure, wrapped in a military-style heavy waxed robe, came to his side without a sound and sat next to him on his makeshift bench.

"Enjoying the quiet?"

"Enjoying the last few moments, Balthasar," replied Marcan. "Wondering what's going to happen today."

"You're going to Demetrian. He'll keep you safe."

"Or I run somewhere further south," said Marcan. "It's cheaper, the food is tasty and I can survive on what you've paid me." He patted Balthasar's knee. "I owe you for your patronage and your protection. I'm sure I was the worst actor you've ever hired."

"But the best Emperor Marcan," said Balthasar. "Anyway,

had I not acted as I did I would have been a worse man than I am. Interrupts my morning routine." Both emitted a single grunt of laughter. Any threat Balthasar had felt was now hidden behind Marcan's boyish profile. "It's time you went back, Marcan. You've made a veteran proud, and in truth, I think maybe I owe you." He passed across a scrap of paper. "Demetrian's address."

Marcan read it without recognition or curiosity. It was just a name from a play.

"Thank you," he said. "I hope neither of them has an old mother in Bistrantium."

"You've come a long way since that first morning," said Balthasar. "You're a different man."

Chapter 17

Demetrian marched down the road. His military gait in a merchant's tunic was a source of humour for his neighbours. Demetrian knew of the conversations that always took place around him but never to his face but he was proud of his guardsman's background. He had protected two of the imperial line–the late emperor and the lost one–and now he was just an instructor for gladiatorial schools and rich merchants' sons. When the Emperor Marcan had disappeared before the summer, all his guards had been dismissed as standard protocol. There was no remorse, no resentment, just shame.

So it was no surprise that the empire's greatest bodyguard knew of the hooded figure following him from the second turn. This district of the capital was new, built in a grid pattern, and only muggers or stalkers made three right turns without hesitation. The time of night meant the former was unlikely, the sky dark and already prickled with cold white stars. His shadow wore a generous dark cloak despite the heat wafting from the sandstone bricks, the hood pulled well over his head to prevent even the slightest glimpse. Not unusual for the capital, where privacy was as cherished as coins, but it was worn with such over-exaggeration that it became a thing of attention.

Demetrian knew the posture, the size and the movement with a startling familiarity. The man didn't try to hide his natural gait or build and Demetrian read the implicit message in this. And so, he led a twisting route back, making sure his tail wasn't being tailed, until they reached the corner of his street and the man walked closer. Demetrian dipped his head in respect.

"My lord," he muttered. The shadows from the hood were as black as the night and Demetrian imagined Marcan's cold eyes soaking in the details of his face, looking for betrayal. A moment passed and Marcan didn't move, his hands somewhere in the depths of his robe. Demetrian made sure to keep his own hands in the moonlight, indicating his fair intent. He leant close to the hood.

"This is where you say something, my lord," he whispered.

He felt like he could hear Marcan smile in the dark.

"Your house," came the reply.

A fly came in, fat and frantic, and woke Marcan up before disappearing out of the window to leave him awake and alone with his thoughts. He lay, examining the rhomboid sunlight on the sandstone at the top of the room. Along with the light came gentle noises of people in the street, dulled by the height of the window and calm of his own senses. The air swirled slightly and for the first time since he came to in that roadside hut . . . he opened his eyes without the usual dew of the morning on his face. Instead, in this room and this quiet, he was at peace with the dry air and the high ceiling.

He closed his eyes, drawing in the scents around him. The floating dust must have snatched most fragrances, but he caught animals and dung from the street, sweat and leather, and warm wine sat on the back of his tongue from the night before. He memorised the sensations as if they were a layer of bricks to rebuild his house. None were new to him, but none held any currency.

Marcan sat up, gently swinging his legs from the bed. He'd swum in rustic company for the summer, and their conversation had always offered a trace of prejudice against the city populace. The urban folk were untrustworthy swindlers and Balthasar had implied their inherent nature was the cause of any disaster. But wasn't he, Marcan, a natural city dweller?

As he stood he ticked off one day in the air. He needed to confront certain painful issues immediately, but he hoped none today.

A bitter brew was on the fire, popping bubbles on its surface as Marcan entered the kitchen. Demetrian stood to greet him, laconically but with due respect. They sat together without a word. Marcan drew in a deep breath through his nose and looked around him, taking in the details of a well-appointed but minimalist kitchen.

"How did you sleep, my lord?"

"It feels strange," said Marcan, "to be called that name."

"But not unfamiliar, I presume?"

"No. Perhaps too many nights on the stage." Marcan listened to chatter from the street for a moment. "Perhaps

I'm fooling myself. Who doesn't imagine themselves an emperor occasionally?"

Demetrian stood, walked to the stove and returned carrying a pot of steaming wine. He sat down and poured two heavy clay cups full of the warm liquid, adding a pinch of salt to each.

"Honestly, sir, you're not alone in this. Everything changes every day. Whether you consider yourself a king or an actor, you're right at least once a week."

Marcan studied him sourly over the rim of his beaker. "Bloody sword masters. Always vainglorious."

"The poets of the warrior class, my lord." They both smiled and dropped to silence.

Marcan opened his hands, examining the fingers and palms of an emperor, wondering what he had used them for in his past life. The distinction between the loyalty of Demetrian and Balthasar and the contempt of the villagers that first morning confused his logic.

"Do you know what happened?" asked Demetrian. "Why you're out here rather than in the royal chambers?"

Marcan shook his head. "No," he said. "Nothing more than Balthasar's gossip. And I don't think I'm ready to know more yet. That all happened to a stranger, and it's broken my life. I need to know more about the Emperor Marcan before I start investigating my fall from grace. But not today. Today, I need to rest and to gather my wits."

Demetrian watched him, reading every small thought that crossed his face.

"I protected the emperor for fifteen years," he said, strangely familiar in a paternal manner. "He has always been and always will be the master I serve. You're safe under my roof."

"Thank you. Let me ask, Demetrian, are my personal concerns just as well protected with you?"

"Within reason," he retorted. "I'm not sure I'm ready to hear too many personal things, sir."

Marcan drew a short smile.

"What if I didn't want to return?"

"What if we needed you?"

"If I am the emperor, I was betrayed and exiled. The people don't care for me. If I'm not, I'm just some drunk who woke up with a beaten-up brain. What responsibility do I owe anyone but you?" He paused, his comment met with a stoic silence. "I don't think I am the right person for the throne. What makes sense is for you and your team to put your time into a better candidate and I'll help as I can," he concluded.

"What makes you think that isn't already the case?"

They stared at each other.

"Because I'm still the emperor. For the moment."

The first day pushed by, then the next, and Demetrian was constantly leaving on errands. People came to the door, where they passed messages or exchanged brief conversations with the master of the house.

Meanwhile, Marcan soaked in more of the city's food and smoke. His body yearned for a level of urban contamination to feel balanced again, and he watched as his farmer's tan wore off. Demetrian had advised him against cutting his hair to keep some difference from his public face, but given his nose and his build and the obvious breeding in his gait, neither of them had any real confidence that he was safe in public for too long.

And so, when he finished his exercises a few days after his arrival, he felt a certain sense of betrayal when he saw new faces in Demetrian's home. He walked through the door from the courtyard, dressed only in waist cloth, his torso covered with sweat and unruly hair. He stopped at the sight of unknown men at the circular table. The most eye-catching of the three was a man with beautifully cropped white hair and fine lips which looked like they couldn't close. His jowls were slim but pronounced enough to be the principal feature on his face. Above them, a pair of intelligent eyes sat either side of an edgeless nose. In all, his presence was one of undisclosed intuition, a private and deep wisdom that was never shared.

Next to him sat a man who made his white-haired companion look young. His face was more of an ugly etching than a human form, its lines and creases intimating the deepest disappointment in all he saw. His watery eyes were diluted further by encroaching cataracts, and his cheeks flushed with broken veins. Eyebrows hung like grass at a cliff's edge, swooping down over collapsed eyelids and soft bags underneath. Of the three, his was not the fanciest cloth but it was the most expensive and this small vanity wasn't missed by Marcan. Perhaps it was intended not to be missed.

The third man sat a little further away from the other two. From his small nose, which rose out to meet the world, to the widely spaced dots of eyes, he was made to repel any intimacy. Marcan could not tell whether this was because of an inherent dislike of everything around him, or the barely hidden desire to be needed.

Marcan had paused mid-step. He made his initial examinations unhurriedly. The trio had heard his approach and they watched him enter. They were surprised, not at seeing him, or his state of undress or lack of grooming. Their amazement was because of his own reaction of defensive enquiry. The three expressions were the same as one he had seen Demetrian wear over the past few days as he disappointed his host with his changed character. What shocked them the most, he wondered—the loss of their idol or the loss of their future benefits?

"Don't introduce your guests yet, Demetrian, let me first get to know them," he said. His host, who had missed the silent exchanges, pivoted from his serving bench. Although the men at the table looked to him, he instead watched Marcan for a moment, amused. Demetrian then turned and continued with the platter he was preparing.

Marcan sat next to the small man, whose forehead burst upwards from his small eyebrows. The man, dressed smartly in a detailed fashion, was caught between moving away from a sweaty beast twice his size and offending his reclaimed lord. The other two appeared humoured by Marcan's intentional choice of seat.

"Gentlemen, be honest with me," he began, "Give me the truth without any royal privilege. Is the world a better place now you have found me?"

"Yes," replied the white-haired mandarin. "The empire needs an emperor."

"It completely depends upon your intentions," refuted the ugly one. He glowered at him with his jade eyes. "What are your intentions, my lord? To reclaim your crown or to disappear into the anonymity of a travelling jester?"

The little man next to him paused. He was uncomfortable having to broadcast an opinion.

"Perhaps Selban's question is better put–which Marcan are we answering? The former emperor of the largest professional army in the world, or the itinerant actor?"

"Which in your view is more valuable to you, given past performance?" asked Marcan, turning to him and lifting a dark arm over the back of his seat. The small man now had to address the armpit or ribcage. He brought out a small linen cloth which he flapped dramatically and placed over his nose.

"Honestly, neither has any long-term value," he said spitefully. "You could have been one of our greatest leaders had you lived up to your legend. Unfortunately, this legend was created before you took the throne, so it didn't include you being you. Your greatest achievement was stopping Ferran from taking charge."

"And how did I do that?"

"You were born first," stated the little man.

"Darcy is a rude man," said Selban, shooting his neighbour a stare. "Sir, what he means to say is that with your inherited power and wealth, with your intelligence and understanding, you were the person to bring us out of the deadlock of the split kingdom. But instead of using your divine abilities for advancing the kingdom, you invested them in palace conspiracies. They are a toxic and addictive hobby which ruins many men, but none so great as yourself until now."

"It seems the other side won," stated Marcan. He paused. "So where were my wise advisors and bodyguards when they sabotaged me?" There was a pause, a rare silence of intelligent men humbled.

"I said yes, the world is a better place because of your return," said the white-haired man. His eyes pinned Marcan's with a straightforwardness which was unsettling but welcome. "Your enemies outmanoeuvred your people, but they did so by using your own negligence. But, my lord, let's not consider their victory to be either complete or appropriate. Little Darcy here can work a thousand stories and rumours into what happened, and Selban can break any allegiances made by gold or threats. But, sir, if a horse bucks then there is rarely anything a jockey can do to save the race. And you, sir, were made to buck."

The impudence riled Marcan and he had to calm himself with long breaths. It was not the same as the cavalier peer status Balthasar had attempted with Marcan. Here, Marcan had been the catalyst to his own downfall and these men begrudged him the fact. If he had admitted to himself that he had dreamed of his return, it was to blessings and compliments, not judgement.

"The horses with the strongest pedigree find the best jockeys, sir," the older man continued. "You had a gifted team who spent their waking hours covering scandals and chasing ghosts rather than rebuilding a broken kingdom."

Marcan stared at the man, words on the tip of his tongue rudely held.

Marcan turned to Demetrian. "Was everyone always this rude to me when I was emperor?" he asked.

"No," replied Demetrian, keeping away from the table. He rested against the counter, arms crossed as he watched the four talk. Something of his stance signified that he wasn't one of this political set.

"What did you mean by your original insult?" asked Marcan.

"Which one?" asked the mandarin.

Darcy answered instead of the old man.

"He's referring to his wasted talents," stated Darcy. He spread his hands out on the table, now unaware of his previous discomfort. "Our throne suffered most in the separation of the two kingdoms. With roughly half of the population came over three-quarters of the military. So, we were blessed and burdened by a powerful fighting army which needed battles. We don't have any wars left to fight, so either we had to find a way to turn soldiers into farmers or we'd go bankrupt. Antron had told the old emperor that he could find enough kingdoms to plunder to last another generation."

"And there aren't any?"

"Of course not," replied the mandarin. "So we're bankrupt within a matter of years."

"Or we go to war. A campaign suits Antron well," added Darcy.

"I was the man to lead the country past Antron and the generals?"

"We all thought that."

"How is his war progressing?" asked Marcan.

"Well, let's take stock of where we are. You've only been missing for a few months. Antron has quickly found that ruling isn't as easy as he thought. By coercing various powerful men into his dirty tricks, he's created a dozen lethal blackmailers who know his treachery to the crown. He'll get his war, but not yet."

"So, I go back to my original question," said Marcan

softly. "Is the world a better place now I am back?"

"If you have the balls and the brains you used to, and you now have humility and wisdom, then yes." Selban again with his bubbling, choleric delivery.

"And what is your recommended next move?"

"Helping our enemies to hang themselves," stated Darcy, pushing away from Marcan's armpit.

"They were never friends," stated Marcan. "So what's keeping them together now?"

"Your head," stated the mandarin.

"Loreticus, I presume," said Marcan with a nod. "Then let's not give them my head, but rather each others'. Find me a way to break this triumvirate and we'll have the throne back."

"Do you want it?" asked Loreticus.

"Yes."

"With all of the problems it brings?"

"Yes. The throne is mine, and all that comes with it." He scanned each in turn again. "Who else is on our side?"

"Of most importance, the Empress Alba. Your wife."

"Oh shit."

"So we need to consider how best to manage that situation," said Darcy.

"Bring her here where there's no-one listening?" suggested Marcan.

There was a moment of quiet before Loreticus replied. "She doesn't leave the palace."

"Ever?"

No-one replied.

"So a reunion, if she'll have you," added Selban. "But that is for Loreticus to arrange."

Chapter 18

Alba sat, stroking the ends of her fingers as if to wipe powder from them. Only Loreticus thought that he knew her well enough to recognise her nerves. People saw in her what they always wanted to–an emperor's daughter, in control of her life, a divine and flawless somebody. Her laugh was to be treasured, and a simple few words delivered in her warm voice were treasured for life, and she would often pander to the needs of people she met. She was the wisest of her family, the most logical and the most devious. He had gone through his career with her father and her husband as she had grown in to this impressive politician. It hurt him as he watched her from the shadows by the tunnel, the princess obsessing over the feelings of a man, who was only an imposter of her husband.

Loreticus had once told her in the height of her deafness, she was idolising a man many times smaller than her. Marcan had written terrible poetry and ignorant love letters, more about himself than her, and she had read them in ecstasy. Just as he had resolved himself to his favourite protégé becoming the wife of an ape, the ape disappeared in to petty intrigue. He left her for the minuscule politics of court, a court which had little external threat and so craved its own internal tension.

Loreticus had told her that given who she was, she could do nothing but marry beneath her. She had told him he didn't always have to prove himself right.

Loreticus had watched as her glowing eyes grew lidded and her heart had stopped. He worried about her depression, worried about how she leapt at the mention of his name in case Marcan had remedied his stupidity.

There was a searing pride in his young friend when she had seen the necessity to save the throne. To cut the apple to get rid of these three, four maggots. But perhaps they had underestimated the rot. He stemmed his nerves; Marcan was back and Loreticus was in control again. In the worst case, he would find a way to massacre those three fools in their shiny armour to stop them hurting her, he thought.

She was his secret weapon. The most underestimated mind in the empire. Given time and influence, she would intimidate even him, he thought.

"I hear that you had your run-in with General Iskandar. Did you tell him who banished Lady Dess?" asked Loreticus as he stepped in to the sunlight. The old spymaster adopted his jolly demeanour, one which implied that all was going to plan.

She nodded.

"Fine," he said. "Have nothing more to do with her. I went to visit her as part of my investigation to find Marcan. You aren't a petty lady, but you might have some solace from her imprisonment. Any ambitions she thought would come from this disgusting little act have been cruelly crushed."

"Horrible little woman," she muttered.

"Horrible!" he echoed with mock femininity. She squeezed his forearm in rebuke. He gave her the smile that he knew she loved, the great grin that shrank his eyes. Slowly, he drew his expression back to its usual look of mild indifference.

"Did she know where he was?"

"No. No more than I did."

"And what of him?" Her tone drew the conversation to the hidden purpose of her invitation. No the utter lack of logic, she kept an immature hope for reconciliation. She must punish this man, who might not even be the original Marcan, for his transgressions. He might not have been guilty of that night with Dess, but she knew in her heart that he was not close to innocent.

Loreticus was quiet for a moment. She wondered whether he was summoning his dramatic genius or his diplomatic tact.

"He's well, humbled, still sharp as a button. You know that he has little recollection of the events."

Alba frowned, quiet.

"Which means that there was likely some drug in his brain," he concluded.

"Which means what? That he was innocent of everything, or that he was too drugged to make his escape?"

"I know him fairly well," commented Loreticus, "and whilst he is not a perfect man he is no lunatic either, unlike his cousin."

"You didn't answer me, my diplomatic friend," she rebuked. "I know you well enough to know that either you'd lie for your empire or you'd lie for the sake of the brotherly union."

"You should treat this as a new start. A new version of Marcan is here. Anyway, I don't think that Marcan was caught mid-adultery that night," he replied. "In my belief, it was staged and badly so. She waited long enough for you to arrive before she ran." He held his hand up to silence her interruption. "Antron and his gang were remarkably unsurprised by events. In fact, the vain little Iskandar didn't show a single jealous pique, which was proof enough for me. He values his status more than his marriage. That means to have been cuckolded should have made him a principal complainant in this matter and he should have punished his wife himself. Instead, he looked more distressed when he learned that Dess was exiled than when she was publicly branded a wicked woman."

"I took pleasure in telling him myself. Perhaps he knew that she was unfaithful but couldn't stop loving her anyway?" she mused.

"Doubtful," responded Loreticus. "I've never seen that gentle a spirit in his bones. He's a man too scared to break."

They walked a little further in silence.

Her garden always fascinated him. It was pristine, the reward of her own hard work, almost flowerless but beautifully colourful and vibrant. Greens of all shades glistened in this little world, with the occasional purple or black leaves offering a thoughtful depth. Tree trunks were elegantly straight or wound around each other like hand-carved columns, all sitting under manicured branches. The air was light around her on these walks and this ethereal sensation wove itself into his memories and fondness for her.

"You've spent time on your garden," Loreticus remarked.

"I've had ample time to spend, Loreticus. You gentlemen are busy tidying up your mess."

He nodded.

"When will you be ready to see him?" he asked.

"Who said that I wanted to? He's been a fool."

Loreticus let that pass. It betrayed the chaos in her.

"When, Alba?"

"Tomorrow," she replied firmly. "Any longer simply means more sleepless nights. Tell him you had to try harder to convince me."

Chapter 19

The palace was a complex labyrinth of disorganised pathways between buildings. It was there to keep all business of state under one roof, and the old emperor had enjoyed its hermetic atmosphere, devoid of the pollution of everyday life.

Marcan had once scurried down the corridors each morning from his living quarters to the administrative court, his royal person the centre of the civilised world, a gaggle of flunkies and clients following behind. Now Loreticus marched down dusty corridors, trying hard to make the echoes of his footsteps as loud as possible.

As he entered the more remote edges of the court building, he turned swiftly down a smaller tributary passage. It drew to a dead end, stoppered by two giant guards in highly polished armour. The pair examined Loreticus for a moment, scanning his figure for weapons and then parted, opening a door as they did so.

There was such little motivation for Loreticus to have brought a sword into the room. He possessed no weapon or form of physicality which allowed him to win a fight against any one of the generals, let alone all three. Loreticus took stock of the trio, again incongruous in this setting without the emperor with them. They were empty, wooden silhouettes brought shakily to life.

"Ah, welcome," said Antron. He was becoming more comfortable in his role now, the parvenu on the balcony now a faint shadow. "The tip of my tail," he said, as if reading Loreticus's thoughts.

Antron's intelligent face was cut by his thick nose and framed by an ugly, low-maintenance haircut. He was still overly conscious of his every gesture, as if they had to live up to the splendour of the room. This was the de facto emperor frantically weaving his nest.

Loreticus corrected himself—it wasn't just the setting, but the juxtaposition of these three together which surprised him. To see Antron communing with Iskandar and Ferran was astonishing. That they pulled this coup off together was unbelievable. He sensed that they had the confidence of winning first blood, but the bonds between them were not yet settled.

Something told him that they hadn't moved much before he arrived. Perhaps his was the meeting that they were most concerned about. He had avoided them and their envoys for as long as possible, but the demand had been made to visit them and so he had come. The lack of bustle and the stale, cold air devoid of fragrance made the room lifeless as he stood, staring back at them.

To Antron's right lounged Ferran, effeminate despite his reputation. He was the wrong blend of royal blood, and wherever he was he conducted himself as a celebrity. Ferran's affected air of boredom was the main characteristic of his long-nosed face, that and his curly blond hair and piglet eyes. But despite the grotesque mind behind the remarkable face, he exuded a tangible sexuality which had most wives in court watching with interest, albeit against their better judgement. He nodded to Loreticus without his usual warmth.

At the far end of the room stood Iskandar, who always shrank into a dull mute when with these two. On his own he could shake rooms with his words but that was a different man. If the other two masqueraded with their breeding, Iskandar impressed with his godly physique. He stood a head higher than Antron, and what skin showed from his brand-new court clothes demonstrated lean athleticism and a graceful movement. With all of his humility, he couldn't hide the intelligence which clipped his words. Iskandar was a young soul, played with by the other two like bullies in the street, and like bullies they both ran when they thought he might hit back.

Loreticus sniffed, more from the discomfort of dust in his nose than for effect, and he sat heavily on the nearest sofa with a thump. Antron lifted two cups of wine from a table and passed one to Loreticus.

"I am not going to wake up with one of your wives, am I?" he asked, sniffing the liquid daintily.

Antron smiled. "Very droll." He sat down on the same sofa, a prelude to upcoming attempts at friendship. Loreticus found his body wanting to shuffle away from the man. "So, he's been found?"

"He has," said Loreticus. "He was with a travelling troupe of actors for the summer. Apparently doing a rather clever impression of himself."

Ferran laughed. "Isn't everyone nowadays?"

"Who would hide him from us?" snapped Iskandar. He turned to examine Loreticus. "Why didn't you just tell us where he was?"

"Do I look like a person who frequents the shows of itinerant artists?" asked Loreticus archly.

Iskandar shrugged.

"You think so? I don't." Loreticus had to be careful not to let his mouth run around these three. He was, if anything, dangerously judgemental. "Gentlemen, I understand your dilemma and you know me well enough. I don't know how I can help your cause, especially as we still have a legitimate emperor somewhere out there."

Something in the atmosphere of the room shifted, and the generals appeared to relax with the spymaster. Iskandar folded into a chair, moving his attention to his hands. Whether or not it was Loreticus's admission of Marcan's existence which settled their resolve, Loreticus didn't know and he didn't like it. He kept quiet, his face remaining unnaturally passive.

"What is it that we can do for you?" asked Antron. His guest surveyed him.

"Antron, you invited me here. It's rather blunt to presume that I walked in with a price in mind."

"Loreticus, you have this look of highbrow self-satisfaction permanently on your miserable old face. I always expect you to know the right answer."

"You think so?" repeated Loreticus petulantly. He regretted his poor humour, but his nerves were building in his chest. "Antron, I'll be open with you. Marcan was no great general, and he was no genius emperor in the making. He was–is–a flawed man, with a tendency to spend hours thinking about only himself. But he wanted to move the empire forward. He can balance our new country better than you three can. Your future for us, your citizens, is constant bloodshed. The fear of military failure. The fear of bankruptcy. A country run by the military will never have an authentic character–it will simply look like every other usurped kingdom. Soulless, paranoid, hellbent on having a fight. We've split from the zealots, and we have an incredibly fragile moment in which we decide who we are going to be. I don't see in this room the people I trust to create that legend." He spread his palms, smiling with his broad grin, as if he were a grocer saying to an irate customer 'Sorry, we're all out of sycophancy today.'

"Loreticus," drawled Ferran, "you're a wise man, we all acknowledge that. But your primary problem is quite simple. Your opinions are too fixed and for a politician, you're too averse to change. You're the type who watches tradesman produce a work of perfection and then offers advice."

Loreticus pursed his lips as if wrestling back a comment. The insight had stung.

Antron stood, his flat stomach levelling with Loreticus's eyes. The soldier was using an old schoolboy trick–the robust athlete intimidating the pudgy scholar. Neither fitted their stereotype perfectly and this lent the general's action a silliness.

"My friend," said Antron, "there are two things you already know despite your arrogant little denial. The first is that Marcan is not healthy for the stability of the state, especially in its newly formed borders. We have a threat to our very existence looming over the mountains, brothers keen on our destruction. Secondly, the people need your talents to protect our entire country rather than one spoiled family." He weighed two empty hands as if they were scales, mimicking Loreticus, and his face assumed an expression of profound and sincere selflessness. The look didn't fit Antron. "The more this uncertainty continues, the more it hampers our leadership and therefore our very country. An invasion by the fanatics would destroy the privacy that we thrive on in the capital. That goes against everything that you seem to value."

Yet another clumsy move by Antron. Loreticus started to feel a dread materialise, as he realised to realise his deepest fear–the court in the control of people who simply didn't have any political wisdom.

"The zealots don't have an army. They won't invade. Scaremongering is not healthy, general."

Loreticus considered the other two sitting patiently with this man. Ferran with his beautiful big nose, and his penchant for kidnapping. The grim Iskandar a prisoner in himself, hirsute as the pent-up pressure drove the hair from his body perpendicularly. There was nothing that these three could offer him which would give him a feeling of confidence.

"Antron, I don't know whether you're looking to make me your friend or your fearful client. At least keep consistent to one façade and I can pretend to react accordingly."

Iskandar tutted and turned his head to look out of the window. Ferran and Antron might recognise the strategic advantage of having Loreticus on board, but to a man who had barged and bullied his way to the top, his skills were too intangible for value.

"Your friends said that you are petulant," stated Antron.

"Did they?"

"Yes," replied the general. "Exactly that word. 'Petulant' because you lost your champion."

"They're correct in their estimation. I find it hard to believe that they both said that, mainly because Selban is rarely that polite."

Antron laughed. "You're right about him. He's a chatty man with a mouth full of vulgarity."

"And yet you seem to be keen to charm my people to your cause."

"If I need your network it will be through you or your people, and until then I shall put on my best smock and dance with you all." He paused, somehow frustrated. "Would you rather we razed everything from Marcan's court and rebuilt? That, of course, is the other option."

Antron glanced at Iskandar, who wore an expression of cynicism.

"Loreticus, your network of influence is necessary to us both at court and in the streets. You were the man the old emperor trusted with his counsel, and ultimately with the smooth ascension of Marcan. That you were unable to keep him out of a scandal is not your fault. He is a waste of your talents. Do you not see that your loyalty to a lost cause is a detriment to the empire?"

"Spymasters always need to keep their loyalty and their wits," rebuked Loreticus gently. "That was the advice of my mentor. And that's why Darcy will make a great spymaster and Selban most likely won't."

Something changed at the mention of Darcy's name and Loreticus watched each quietly. So these men felt confident about Darcy's treachery. The spymaster prayed that he himself wasn't suffering another extended bout of hubris.

"I like you, Loreticus," stated Ferran. He stood, the length of his legs and his spine drawing attention as they uncurled as easily as snakes. "But we know each other well enough to understand our options now that Marcan is back on the scene. Those men of mine who have been stamping around behind you will butcher you and your guard in the street. Marcan will be thrown into a ditch and his assassination blamed on you and whichever of your dirty, little spies refuses to join us. The alternative is to make this work. To create stability and strength in the kingdom. To find a way to regain the zealots' territory."

He hadn't moved nearer to Loreticus, and remained behind Antron. There was no doubt, however, that the lazy, spoiled cousin was the real power in this group. Loreticus smiled, seeing at last why they had managed to get this far.

"Then let's be upfront," replied Loreticus. "What is it that you want, what are you offering and what is it that you recommend I do?"

"Are you going to start working for the generals?" asked Pello. His eyes, at the best of times slightly unfocussed on the physical world, were now scrutinising his master's face for some response.

Loreticus brushed dust from the top of his desk and looked over at his assistant, whose desktop was the polar opposite of his own. Pello seemed to collect paper and he built short, precarious columns of inked sheets. There was a complex and somehow intimidating mixture in Pello, which brought together the guileless and the commanding. There were areas in which he excelled – logic, presumption, memory and finding the only true connection between random events – but his ability to predict human emotions was impoverished.

"No, Pello, we'll not be joining the generals. They were useful tools but now they are becoming rather dangerous."

"To us?"

"To the whole country, my boy," Loreticus retorted. "Never worry about us. Always worry about the empire."

"Doesn't that presume a certain over-confidence about the results of other people's action? Why are you so certain that Antron and Iskandar wouldn't bring in a new stability? Perhaps the most obvious thing to do is to take control of our neighbours."

"Maybe. I could be wrong, but I don't think so. You are too young to realise the cost of such wars, the violence that intoxicates the cities and towns of both countries as the other people struggle with the new rulers. We've been through that and I can tell you flatly that Antron does not have the brains to manage such a strategy."

"Does Iskandar?"

"He does, but he doesn't have the personality. Yet."

"Loreticus," began Pello slowly. "What you're implying is that we don't have anyone."

"We do. When we get Marcan back on the throne."

"Marcan is dead. I know that you've told the other people something else, but I saw it in Demetrian's face and I heard it in the way you talk. I don't understand why you'd want someone on the throne who isn't legitimate."

"Pello, he would be legitimate if Alba, myself and Demetrian said so."

Pello didn't look pleased. He watched as the boy pinched his mouth with his fingertips, looking at Loreticus and then away, then back.

"Because the new Marcan is better?"

"Yes, because he's better."

"How?"

"Because we could manage him more closely. An emperor is the pinnacle of the court, not a ruler on his own. Take the complex history away, and you have a man who can broker the deal we need with the zealots."

Loreticus reached over to his pipe, which he had cleaned needlessly three or four times already that morning. He began to clean it again, then instead packed it full of a leaf which would help him to relax.

"How much did you have anything to do with his disappearance in the first place?" asked Pello.

"Who?"

"The original Marcan."

"I had nothing to do with that murderous plot," stated Loreticus firmly and puffed on the flame in his pipe bowl.

"Who gave the guards extra leave that night?" Pello enquired.

Loreticus stood up.

"Don't follow this route, Pello. I am guilty of many things, and I just don't want to revisit them as I explain life in court to you. There is no start and no end to this. We're just a stretch of the stream and you need to learn not to try to find the ancient spring because it will certainly be far away. Or it might simply not exist."

Chapter 20

Marcan was thinner and grizzlier, and he felt unprepared as he walked through her door. He had started to compare himself to that beaten man in the hut in Bistrantium, as if he were the perfection of the Emperor Marcan. Gone were the darkly charming eyelashes, the sharply edged nose, the thick arms. Instead, here stood a different soul in the same body. Skinnier, calmer, more perceptive. More dangerous.

For moments after he arrived in her ante-chamber, Alba was ill at ease, constantly changing her seat or her posture. She smoothed the material of her dress across her lap.

"I don't understand," she said. "Why are you angry with me?"

Marcan had taken the seat next to her, contrite and ungainly. His mouth and cheeks crinkled and pursed as thoughts came to him, reactions he couldn't control. Remorse was the strongest emotion in his body, not guilt.

"Well, you could call me an idiot, a bloody imbecile," he replied. "That is what I want you to do."

She laughed. "Of course it is. Then it's resolved for you

but just the start for me." She got up, and he stood quickly next to her. "No. You're not getting off the hook quite so easily."

Alba walked a little and he followed, one step behind her.

"Is it true that you can't remember anything?"

"Nothing. Certain faces or things create strong emotions, but I have little else from before. My memories are coming back. Then some things need to be taught before I remember them as true. It's a humbling experience."

"Do you remember me?" she asked flatly.

"Yes. I think so. I think I saw your eyes once in someone else. They were only there for a moment, but it scared me with how little I knew. I see you now and I remember you."

"Do you remember what we had?"

"I believe so. I don't know how I could forget. What people seem not to realise is just how much effort it would take to pretend I'd forgotten everything that I have. It's painful keeping up with knowing whether I knew something in the first place or not." Marcan stopped her and regarded her again, seeing her nerves. She was nothing like the maid in the village. Loreticus had told him many times that he was the lucky one in this relationship. She was the brighter, the one who was remembered for the right reasons. "Was I really that great an idiot?"

A glance came from the corner of her eye, assessing his honesty. She shrugged.

Everything felt like a bitter compromise of her pride, regardless of his intentions. Had the shoe been on the other foot, he would have extracted himself from the situation and would have nursed his pride.

Marcan was here, in her garden, within touching distance of her, and her fondness radiated despite everything that he had done. Even though he was innocent, how could he explain to her why he had vanished for so long? He felt phoney when he tried to explain his forgetfulness, and every time he opened his mouth he sounded like a liar. She turned away from him, and he blamed his ineptitude.

Marcan studied her back and saw that it was perfect; the curve, the skin, the memory of her scent. He wanted to hold her again, not from desire but for comfort. Below the guilt, he felt detached from his normal coarse self with her, as if his head were above water because of her. He thought that there could not be such a fool in the world who would risk losing Alba for a reckless night in someone else's bed.

Her head turned and he saw the curve of her lip. A heavy but small lip, which acted like a purse's clasp to keep her voice and thoughts permanently locked away until she was ready to spend. How he envied that ability, when all he expected himself to do was babble.

"If the world were different," he asserted flatly, "I would win your heart again. I would make your hopes real, I would make you happy again. If the world were different, I would hold you whenever you felt alone, whenever you had a bad dream, whenever you felt cold. We would live on a beautiful farm away from drama. We would read and plant, cook and laugh. If it were different, I would love you as you deserve to be loved."

Her head had lifted as if to hear better and turned in his direction. Eyes, cool with old hurt and a broken promise.

She surveyed him as if he had just offered a deal in the market.

"But it's not different, is it?" she said. "Otherwise you wouldn't need to define it as 'different'. You have the choice, Marcan, to change your life. You've had no better opportunity to do so than right now. If you wanted to leave the politics far behind, you could–we could. But the world isn't different and none of your unprepared, schoolboy poetry will change that. Look, Marcan, let me be frank. Marriage didn't answer my questions, but it certainly gave me somewhere to devote my efforts."

"I was emperor once, and I shall be again. I know that I have an unfinished fate in this palace, on the throne. At this moment, the empire needs stronger and wiser leadership than it has. That was your father's choice, and returning was my choice."

"No, Marcan, don't use a dead man's intentions to support your own petty ambition. If you want to continue playing politics, then be candid enough to say so. My father wanted you to be powerful and peaceful, and he wanted me to be happy. Because of you, he would be frustrated in both.

"We could find a beautiful estate tomorrow with vineyards, but I doubt that you want that dream to become true any more than you want us to have a traditional marriage. You must realise, Marcan, that I will always be the fields and the hills of our empire, and you'll always dream of the sea beyond our borders." She studied him, her lips clipped tightly shut again. She willed his face to be familiar, and now she saw again the generous family nose and the wily eyes. The lips that were thin one moment and swollen the next. He was nothing but a boy waiting for permission to go play.

"Come back tomorrow," she said.

Marcan emerged through the thick door into the patchy sunlight. The height of the wall dwarfed his bulk and his hood threw his face into shadows. He strode across without seeming to look up, gliding between the other hooded pedestrians, and came to a stop in front of the table.

"Gentlemen," he said, almost as a statement rather than a greeting.

They both nodded. Loreticus took a deep breath.

"It seems that you are going to be leaving on another sabbatical," he said. "Your three old duelling partners are about to get involved in your life again. They know you've been found and they're asking for help from people they'd previously not dared to approach."

"Let's be clear–I wasn't exactly found. I came back to the capital on my own, remember? Do I need to know details of what the generals are up to?"

Loreticus let the man's brovado sit. Marcan's greatest ability had always been to rework history and believe the more convenient version. "I don't know their exact plans. I do know that we should leave as soon as possible."

"Tomorrow afternoon," replied Marcan.

"Not soon enough," said Selban.

"That's soon enough. I have an appointment tomorrow morning which I cannot miss."

Chapter 21

The management of markets in the city was constantly the fuel of discussion and debates. The main stretch of stalls by the palace went on for at least two miles, taking up the centre of the city three days a week. It effectively blocked any urgent foot traffic except imperial business and even then, the guards had to rattle their shields or prodded with their spear tips to get through.

Some merchants and traders complained of the violence and crime. Buyers complained because the market had no set zones. If you needed to buy a basket or bread, you might have to walk the entire length of this bustling ecosystem to find a competitive price. Lucky merchants loved the layout, many with stands held for generations.

Marcan had been shocked the first time he arrived back in the capital and entered the tangle of stalls. The smells of meat on coals, baked bread and blood on stone from the butchers mixed with sweat, perfumes and fresh leather. Flies moved in swarms, orbiting the food stalls and annoying the hooded masses as they sloped past bare-faced traders.

Shouted promotions, bantering cries and mock insults flew between the regulars. The sombre brown cloaks of Marcan's clique faded amongst the blues and the yellows of the merchant classes, the black cloaks of the visiting religious men and the white of the city officials. Soldiers in private or public pay loitered by the food stands. The trio weaved through disorganised lines of stalls, their pyramids of fruit or spices piled in the shade.

Selban led them under a domineering building, a covered part of the bazaar. He swung to one side, dragging the others without comment, and all three stood back in the shadow of a merchant selling piles of chains. They waited, breath silent, their strange postures encouraging the stall owner to ignore them. A small group of seemingly random pedestrians coalesced by one of the four exits, in eyesight of the trio. They stood a little too close for strangers and then one began to make a series of gestures with his hand, indicating to different figures within the group. The gaggle split, two retracing their steps back towards the palace whilst the other pair headed east in the direction of the wealthier neighbourhood.

Selban started again, leading them out of the nearest doorway and into the throng. Marcan saw murder in every turn of a hood, and people began to crowd him. The sun covered everyone in a sticky and odorous sweat, and flies and dust made an effort to blind everyone. Marcan felt nauseous, jostled, unable to find control or sanity within this melee. A pain throbbed in his upper spine, his stomach rose up through its tubes to his mouth and suddenly his limbs shuddered.

Loreticus snatched at Selban's sleeve as soon as he caught

sight of Marcan's pallor. They darted between shoulders of passers-by, the older men taking the falling emperor and catapulting him through the crowd. Loreticus let Selban lead, keeping one hand firmly around Marcan's bicep and the other on the hidden hilt of his knife. He knew that they were tiring–it was a long time since either he or Selban had been in active physical shape. Marcan was lurching, chin down as if drunk. Five, ten minutes they powered through the throng, Loreticus thinking only of each step, in time, forgetting all else but vigilance for the assassins. Then the people started thinning in concentration, the air noticeably cooled and the trees came back to prominence, casting cold shadows on to the thoroughfare. Selban slowed, to catch his breath, then yanked at Marcan and dragged the three of them onwards again, down an alley between the houses, the coolness of the dark mitigating the midday heat. He made a motion with his hand for Loreticus to remain with the emperor and he slunk out of the shadows as a figure came into sight. Selban stepped forward, as if to pass the man and jabbed frantically against the man's leg, his arm straight. There was a pitiful yelp, and Selban rammed the figure away, out of sight of Loreticus in the alley.

Selban took up speed again, dragging the other two with him. Loreticus looked behind but saw no silhouettes following them. He turned to look forward and saw a long, thin stiletto blade in Selban's hand, gleaming darkly with someone's blood.

Selban turned, turned again and then stopped, looked behind them and knocked on a servants' entrance with his boot. It opened and the trio vanished into the buttery smell of a kitchen. The room was warm from the morning's baking but empty other than the giant who had let them in. He stood back, settling a thick baton against his hip and looked distantly over their heads.

Selban looked up and said, "This is my spare house. Normally rented but luckily free at the moment." He looked vexed by his statement.

Loreticus peered up at him quizzically as they settled Marcan into a chair.

"Sorry," said Selban, "money matters. Of course - more pressing problems and all that." He collected Marcan's lolling chin in his hand and opened one of his eyes with a thumb. "Smelling salts," he ordered the guard. "Cold water for the patient and some wine for the old men."

The colossus moved off with a surprisingly quiet step, slipping into a corridor in a dim corner of the kitchen.

Marcan started to move, a grease exuding from his white cheeks.

"Grumbling gods, my eyes hurt," he said, pressing his palms against his face.

"Are you sick?" asked Selban, touching the back of his neck like a doting mother. He realised his awkward gesture and drew away, wiping his hands on the proffered cloth from the returning guard. Loreticus was watching Selban rather than the slumped figure in the chair. Selban's obsequious nonsense amused more than annoyed him. Eventually, the host caught his eye and he stood, his loose jowls coming to a quiet stop. He jutted out his chin in rebuke.

Loreticus made a gesture for patience and to leave Marcan alone. They went together to the long table, which bore hundreds of cutting scars from years of meal preparation.

"That isn't a sickness," said Loreticus under the sound of the wine spilling into his cup. "That was panic. I've seen it in young soldiers in a fight when they rapidly realise where they are." He passed a full cup to Selban.

"Are we in trouble?"

"I don't know."

"You're making me feel like I've made a bad bet."

Loreticus drank deeply. His answer came a little too late, perhaps intentionally. "Of course not. He's only just back." And then he turned, looking directly at Selban. "I realised where I had seen that motif of Dess's family before. There was an urn with her at the red fort. It looked rather new if my memory holds. Has she lost anyone recently?"

"Not that I remember," replied Selban. "She and Iskandar were out of the city for four or five seasons not so long ago. He was leading the military campaign behind the river, then leading the army along the new borders. Perhaps it pertains to that."

"A sibling? A cousin? Her last lover?"

"Only child, no close cousins. Why would she take it with her?"

"Must be a lover then. No wonder Iskandar sacrificed the scheming wench if she has form enough in the past. The woman's a veteran of this sort of thing."

They turned to look at the stooped figure of Marcan. His face turned to them, hearing their emotional whispering.

"Hello there!" smiled Selban, raising a glass. Loreticus had to turn his back at the dismal melodrama of the cry, his eyes rolling.

"Better," grumbled Marcan. "What happened?"

"Oh, the heat, the press, and so on. Most likely you have a touch of a fever as well." Selban went over, his gait that of a family nurse. "You're safe now. Let's work out what's next."

"Next step," stated Loreticus gruffly, "is for the boy to sleep for the day. He can keep his appointment tomorrow morning and then he is out of the city."

"Where to?" asked Marcan. "And you do realise that I'm not a boy? I'm almost middle aged."

"Everyone looks like a youth to Loreticus," sniggered Selban. "He was born an old man with an old man's eyes."

"You're going somewhere safe," said Loreticus. "To stay with a friend outside the city."

"Don't you think that I should know?"

"No. There's no disrespect intended, but I think it's better that you find out when you find out. That way there aren't any whispers and certainly no opinions for me to tidy up."

Alba was more formal early the next morning, if somewhat more accepting of his presence. This time her hand servant was frequently present, seemingly without any mischievous intent, and the lady herself was relaxed and met him in the gardens of the palace. There was a strange, cloying sense of fondness in Marcan's chest, the shape of a feeling which had lived there before.

Loreticus had told him that he was grieving for his old life, but Marcan didn't believe him. This sadness was something else. He was looking in on a world that he had once valued so dearly but now realised was fundamentally sordid.

"I thought about you the entire night," he said earnestly. "I don't have all of my memories back yet, but I realise that whatever we had was wonderful and then broken. I'm sure it was my fault. I can't remember why, but I'm sure it was."

"It was," she stated. "My tutor used to tell me that a person's character was never consistent. There is a central part, the heart, which remains anchored. The rest of it is like a cloud, drifting in the direction of whichever person they are talking to at that time. You were always trying to be busy and you drifted a lot. Too much."

Alba spoke in concepts as a rule, rarely offering a specific instance for him to interpret. "I gave myself to you, without regret and without concern. You were just an honest soldier then. It was the politicking that made everything a mess."

They were walking and she kept a step ahead. He watched her through the pale dress she wore; occasionally her figure was illustrated by sunlight catching through the thin material.

Marcan was spellbound by her. Her neck rose so gently from her shoulders, too thin to be able to hold her hair, which was thick and deep brown. When she ducked to look at a broken leaf or a young seedling, he spied that bottom lip and it made him tremble with a memory he couldn't find.

The old emperor had designed every aspect of the garden with cryptic shapes. All the little tricks that he had employed, thought Marcan, all the energy he spent scheming.

Alba was talking about something, but he was watching her without thought. She stopped and turned and he had to gather his wits. Had she asked a question? By her expression, it seemed so. Desperately, he looked for an escape route.

"Have I been in these gardens before? They seem familiar."

She watched him, looking for guilt.

"Yes," she said. "They were your gardens for a long time."

"They don't feel familiar to be in, just they seem. . . . . not strange."

He was lying. She was watching his expression with distaste.

"I sometimes get panicked by what I've forgotten."

"I'm sure it will pass," she said coldly. He looked up at her, but before their eyes met she begun to move forward again. They retreated into an older corner of the garden, one intentionally untouched by the emperor's hand. He had once used it as a deep green oasis to disappear from the court, to drop his mantle as leader of the empire, and he would sit and find his childishness again. It was nothing, a small square of thirty paces by thirty, three sides bricked up, but for him it was the unkempt heart of the garden. Roses ran along the walls and potted plants in broken amphorae sat in various spots. In the centre of the square was a small, tiled pool with water shaded a fine pale blue.

Alba slipped off her shoes and sat down, letting her feet slide into the water. Marcan at first poised himself half-heartedly on a bench, a certain shyness cramping his legs, but then he joined her. The air turned cold. Something changed in his heart as he sat there, and it shaped the direction of his thoughts. His destiny was real, and it was manifesting itself now. He sat as the cohort of the imperial princess, alone, intimate, mere weeks after sleeping in fields and eating burnt meat off the bone. A quiet confidence rose in him, a stain which was now indelible as it was no longer faith but real. He smiled silently, lifting his chin up.

With an otherworldly *oip*, a raindrop tumbled heavily into the pool. The breeze shifted again as the trees woke up to the clouds and breathed in the scent of rain. *Doip oip oip*. The rain was cool and the air warm. They sat, postures mimicking each other, close but not touching, unable to concentrate as they waited for the smallest thing to spoil it. The rain felt like a fresh sheet had been thrown across the garden, the grass and gravel fizzing and crackling from a hundred thousand contacts.

"What next?" she asked. He knew that she wanted to hear that he would be back the next day, and had he been a braver man, he would have agreed. But he had to follow his fate.

"I leave." She closed her eyes, turning her face to the clouds. Marcan watched then did the same, jumping slightly every time a fat drop slapped him. "I don't know how long for, or where to. But it won't be forever and it will be somewhere safe. Do you want to come with me?"

"No," she laughed. "I'm safe enough here and you would be endangering both of us by taking me. You know that I've learned that all advice is bad. All of it. The only thing that they should have ever told me was that life will often be sad, but more often it will be beautiful." The water ran from her forehead, over her damp hairline and down her pale temples. "Marcan, don't worry about me. I am vindicated. No more do I feel like the victim, or the fool. No more do I feel like the romantic adolescent. I am happiest when I am on my own, as I always was as a child. Even more so now without that onerous expectation of marriage. The world would always be for you men of politics, born and designed to thrive either in your little huddles of power or on the battlefield, and only amongst yourselves. I don't blame you, Marcan."

He waited for a moment, feeling the rain drape itself like a sheet over them both. And then when it was uncomfortably cold for him, he stood. Alba hadn't moved, her face lifted, her eyes closed.

He bent, feeling like a thief, and stole a kiss, expecting her to move away from him. Instead she accepted his lips, the roughness of his chin on her perfect cheek, the loneliness in his touch. He wouldn't ruin the moment, so he stood and briskly walked away, through the garden, through the corridors, between Loreticus's guards by the door and out, blessed now for the coming battle.

Chapter 22

Darcy sat with his usual edginess in the foyer of the ancient complex, grouped with the daily clients of Ferran. There was something demeaning for him being amongst these money men and soldiers in their second career. His leg bounced erratically, and he felt his fine features and balding pate mark him as somewhat less masculine than these back-slapping apes.

His was a world of favours, subtle cajoling and out-and-out blackmail. It wasn't an environment of pleading for as much as you could and being grateful for it. Outcomes for him were black and white; only the means changed. The opposite was true for his peers in the waiting room and it felt to him as if he spoke a different language or was a different race.

Ferran came through the doors without any pomp. He slipped through, two enormous guards in polished mail behind him, and looked around the room. The clients had fallen silent, pivoting towards the great doors which had admitted petitioners to the noble family for generations past. It was akin to being in a place of religious worship. Ferran caught Darcy's eye and waved him in, turning without waiting to see whether the small man had seen or reacted.

Darcy pushed through the clumsy crowd, grumbling as his expensive material smudged on some lesser apparel or caught on someone's belt buckle. He popped out of the front line, scampering the dozen or so paces to the open doors.

He had not been in this ancient home before. It wasn't somewhere one tended to visit, unless you were a client like those outside, or a whore, a mercenary, a butcher or a wine merchant coming after hours. The room was much more austere than he had imagined. It was rectangular, with natural light from an open end, which led to a small garden, and a long aperture in the ceiling which ran almost the entire length. On the floor were mosaics of insignias belonging to families who had married into the dynasty. The nearest were pale from being worn by footfall over the seasons. Ferran stood by a strategically placed table, dramatically lit by the downward sun. On the table, silver jugs and carafes held the horizontal light from the garden and spread it around their girth. The ubiquitous pot of rock salt sat on one end.

"The Noses through the ages," laughed Ferran in his drawl, gesturing with his arm. Ancestors were caught in acts of honour, battle or seduction in painted panels on the walls. Almost all had had their beak exaggerated. Darcy looked, interested in the depth of history in the room, and Ferran appeared proud that a man like Darcy was taken by his inherited vanities.

"You must hate this routine," said Darcy, his eyes still on the panels. "All of this beautiful family allusion only to open the doors to a bunch of peasants asking for things." He turned to accept the cup from Ferran's extended hand. A black wine rolled around inside, soaking up the shadows in the room.

Ferran shrugged, moving back to the open end of the room. Darcy found himself following without being bidden, obeying without being told to. They sat and Ferran leant forward.

"I do what I am expected to do," he explained. "I have more duties than anyone I know, with fewer aspirations. Keep the family alive, marry well, have a few sons, support whoever is on the throne."

"We always presumed that you wanted the throne for yourself," said Darcy, leaning heavily on a straight arm to silence his bouncing knee.

"Why?" laughed Ferran. "I'm of the blood, I'm comfortable and I don't want any more responsibility."

"But you're the only one of the royal blood left."

"Well, that's not strictly true. There's my cousin Marcan and there's Alba."

"I thought that Marcan was soiled and is planning to flee the kingdom."

"Still alive."

"But no threat to you."

Ferran rocked on his buttocks, rising on to tiptoes and then letting his feet fall flat.

"And that's why you've decided to put your bets on me?" he asked.

The garden was being tended by two slim middle-aged servants, both wearing the ankle strap of slave status. Few families were legally allowed to own slaves in these modern times, and many of those who still did had used religious authority and so left in the exodus. Ferran's clan, being a family of state, was always entitled to own slaves and it would have been almost improper for them not to have them.

"Where does Antron fit into this little scene of the new Emperor Ferran?" asked Ferran. "Did your crack team of squirrelling schemers think of that issue?"

Darcy winced at the patronising comment.

"Just me," he said. "Not Selban. Not Loreticus."

"Just you?"

"The others are proud and principled men; by which I mean that they are more lawyers than realists. In my mind, the most likely outcome is that Antron assumes control of the state but he is not a royal. You should take the throne and let him run the country."

"A bold recommendation. A dangerous one to be spoken so calmly."

"You have a valid claim. More so than anyone else."

"Darcy, I didn't mean dangerous for me," stated Ferran flatly. "Besides, you're asking me to be a puppet prince."

"As a ruler with a wise counsellor."

They watched the gardeners for a moment, Ferran's silence giving them breath from a rather awkward path of conversation.

"And why should I not be the wise one?"

"Would you like more clients and petitioners nagging you?"

Ferran laughed. His colourful, sharp eyes glanced around at a home familiar to the point of claustrophobia. Ten years ago, he had been riding at the head of a eager and active army, and this had been a peaceful home to return to.

"As simple as that, eh? And why do you presume that Antron will accept it?"

"That is a discussion to be had. But of the two conversations–with you or with him–which was the logical one for me to have first?"

Ferran nodded, his face calm. That he was listening was a positive sign and Darcy sat up slightly straighter, pushing ahead with his momentum.

"Of course, for this to happen and for us to make your assumption easier than Antron's, you need to stop antagonising friends and enemies."

Ferran turned, pivoting his palm on his knee to look directly at Darcy.

"Could you explain a little more?"

"Well, stop stealing people. Every host puts their second-best cook in the kitchens when you visit in case you like the food and decide to kidnap him. The old emperor had to station an extra garrison of rangers on the border to try to head off your raiding trips into the zealots."

Ferran laughed. "I'm a collector," he said. He pointed at the gardeners. "The best temple garden attendants from the new country." He gestured to a door in the far corner which appeared to be a small kitchen. "The best personal cook in the kingdom." He continued indicating doors and people out of sight. "The best cartographer from the northern tribes. The most beautiful daughters of the barbarian kings. The wisest philosophers from the islands." He turned and regarded Darcy again. "This is a divine environment. Nowhere else on earth will you find a community so close to perfection as this."

"They're all slaves," replied Darcy. "Doesn't that somehow dim their minds?"

Ferran shook his head, and it seemed he hadn't heard the judgement in Darcy's voice. "After a few months, they realise that there won't be any violence or escape. When they are used to their new lives, they begin to contribute with whatever they have."

He drank deeply.

"You understand my point though, even if it was made badly? As an aristocrat, you have a certain protection, but as head of state you would cause a war if you went raiding."

"Of course, I understand what you are asking for."

"Stability for trade. Wealth for the country."

"A royal emperor like the country deserves," laughed Ferran, and he drained his cup.

Chapter 23

Dess was waiting outside again when Loreticus was shown in. This time, they sat on the terrace which looked out to the dry hills, raised high up above the dirt storeys below. He had decided to call on her without warning, but she had recognised his carriage as it approached.

Even without notice of his arrival, she was still beautiful, still elegant, still threatening. But there was a little less care in her arrangement, as if she no longer valued her appearance as much. With its ugly and barren slopes, this countryside was certainly not a place to breed optimism and hope.

"I brought you a small library this time," he said as he entered.

Just like his late wife, Dess was easy to make smile, thought Loreticus. He wondered whether this transparency of spirit lent Dess the same humility.

"Thank you," she said gently. "When I heard that you had arrived, I thought that it was with a couple of butchers. Close off a dirty secret to protect the emperor."

"Well," he said, lost for words for a moment.

"It's a beautiful view," she continued. The hills were rolling, dun, a canvas for shadows from the clouds and each other. She ignored the rocks, the scree clattering across dusty undulations. "I hated it when I first arrived. Now I find it perfect."

"He's not the emperor anymore," stated Loreticus. "Nor is it a secret anymore."

She turned to him. "That surprises me," she said. Loreticus felt himself becoming tense, the side of his body closer to her going rigid at the thought of her erratic temper. With surprise, Loreticus realised why powerful men fell in love with Dess. He had always assumed that it was due to some dark seduction that she plied. It wasn't. It was because she was raw and worthy of protection.

"Well, it was quite the spectacle," he said, staring out over the fort's wall. "You did plan it well."

She fell quiet, looking at the side of his face for a moment and then turned away.

"When you come to kill me," she said indolently, "no blood and no pain, please. Don't make me become an item of gossip."

"I won't kill you," he replied. "I think if those orders were to be given, they would have been sent already. I just think that they don't know what to do with you now."

"Wonderful," she said sardonically. "The punishment of purgatory. But you do know that ultimately the result will be the same? There are too many secrets yet to be revealed to allow me to float around the palace or the court."

"I don't understand," Loreticus said, this time turning to her to better understand her implication. "Are there things that I don't already know about?"

"Loreticus," she laughed, "how manly of you to presume you knew even the half of what I talk about at court with my friends."

He smiled, admonished. Of all his sins pride was the greatest.

"It seems that they have won though. The generals are in command," he said. "Your protectors hold the reins."

"No. Until Marcan is dead, I have my stay of execution. Once his body is delivered, my story will be closed in only one possible manner."

Years of hard conversations had not prepared Loreticus for this interaction. He was far too involved in her case, with her fate. He had nominally dismissed his focus due to the importance of this intrigue–a fight for the throne itself–but with very little reflection, he knew that it was because of his attraction to this woman. Again, he glanced at her. She was looking away from him, her golden hair reddening in the sun, the corner of her jaw running in a perfect line to her unseen chin. The neck that wore naked muscle and a pulse through the metallic bronze skin. He could feel the heat coming off her shoulders, and for some reason he felt this warmth in his lips from afar. Eyes closed, he turned his head to his lap and made to stand.

She heard him, moving elegantly to meet him. As she rose, her dress fell forward to offer the briefest glimpse of a perfect tanned breast. It happened so quickly that he did not look away, nor realise the event until after she was standing. She had not noticed, but a look on her face signalled that something had happened to his own expression.

"What?" she asked softly, startled.

"Nothing," he said with guilt in his chest.

"You know, Loreticus, next time you visit you're actually going to have to tell me why you come. You don't believe that I know where he is. You don't think he'll come to rescue me. And you don't think that I'll reveal any great secret about Iskandar and his wooden-headed chums."

Loreticus folded his arms and stared at the floor for a few breaths.

"Maybe I shall be able to explain next time," he said slowly.

As he walked down, out of the house, away from her and the setting sun, away from the dry fountain and the dusty plants, he looked for the funeral urn. It stood where the salt had on his last visit, in a prime place in the middle of the foyer, proudly displaying its pearled swallow insignia. He stared as he passed it, connecting it silently with what he had just seen.

Much as he held the memory of that stolen intimacy, it was confused by the black necklace of bereavement which draped hidden underneath the dress. Who had she lost? Loreticus felt ice run in his veins as he considered the possibility that Dess knew that the true emperor was dead.

Chapter 24

Ten of them left before dusk, out of the gate on the road to the new borders at the base of the mountains. The structure was massive, imposing and built to inspire the thousands of soldiers who marched towards the boiling horizon. The gate stood as a tangible threat to those fanatics squirming in their pits and their prayers the other side of the mountains. Its great, bleak majesty held firm against the evening sun, its unusual grey brick squared and sharp with perfect shadows.

After the gate came a long, artificially smoothed slope which evolved the corda as it stretched like an arrow shaft in the direction of the borders. The horses slowed their gait on the gradient, and they were forced to weave continuously by the crowds returning to the city for nightfall. The party eventually broke free from the numbers as the ground flattened, and the horses snorted in relief. Turning back, Marcan saw that the gate was dwarfed by the overall structure, a massive grey line challenging the mountains themselves. Millions upon millions of bricks blocked the view of the city, crowned by regular torches and silhouettes.

"You built that façade," commented Selban, bouncing and jerking slightly in his saddle. Marcan continued to stare at it, twisting in his saddle until he felt his mount complain. The darkness had snuck in without him noticing, and when he turned back from the glow of the city he was momentarily blinded in the plum darkness.

"Interested in where we're going?" asked Selban, prompting a conversation. Marcan had tired of the man quickly over the last day, and decided that it would be a long journey if he was polite.

"No," he said.

He watched the ripe, coloured clouds as they strained against the mountains' summits. The peaks had torn some cottony underbellies, and now the clouds shed immense diagonal slants of rain.

These were divine threats to a man of the empire, and Marcan felt a knot of anxiety growing inside him. His birthplace, the kingdom, rarely saw heavy rainfall and sat in a dry plateau, harvest-fed by the damper farm lands days away from the capital. No civilian ventured out here to the new borders, and any legions sent here came back complaining of the constant cold, winds, rains and rocky grounds. Maybe this wasn't the edge of the known world, but it was certainly the edge of the desired world.

Ten years ago, Talio and his religious extremists had brokered peace with the exhausted old emperor, who had spent years beating the barbarians in to submission. When he returned to claim that dream of rest that borne him through the final, brutal seasons, the emperor found blood on the streets of his home town. He sold his dignity after a weak resistance, giving Talio a land of his own. And so when the zealots had claimed the other side of the mountains as their own, the emperor laughed and offered them carts. "Take the land!" he had cried. "I might not have brought you to heel, but those wild gods in the mountains will. May you get thinned out on the way through and we'll not see you again!"

This last compromise in a life of conflict and betrayals had broken the old emperor. He had kissed his daughter Alba's hand as he gave her away to the unblemished young hero Marcan. Then he settled into his palace and his gardens and his self-enforced ignorance.

The horses beneath Selban and Marcan plodded along, flicking their ears to the shifting underside of the clouds. If these vast, disembodied creatures guarded the mountains so that neither animal nor man should pass through, surely Loreticus could find a more logical hiding place?

Eventually, Loreticus led the party to a cleft in the drumlin under the slopes. To the eye, there was nothing but a dark patch of lake and the striped shadows of the rising ground, but as they approached something warm penetrated the thick, cold air. Two buildings stood solid and white, glowing in the dusk against the deep purples and blacks. One was a family cottage, chimney rising proudly from its end whilst its companion structure was a much bigger, bolder manor house of a poor architecture. Behind the building rose a sharp, wooded slope and behind the cottage the valley disappeared into gloom.

The party arrived five minutes too late to miss the first few frosty spatters of rain. The unexpected drops gave energy to the horses' gait and they instinctively found the stable doors at the base of the bigger building. Everyone moved in quickly, the icy water rooting through their clothes, finding paths under their collars.

The men dismounted in silence and Loreticus gestured to Demetrian that he and his guard would spend the night with the animals. Selban and Marcan followed the spymaster's dark shape, flexed into a comical bird pose with his hands on the back of his hips and his elbows squared out like wings. The ride had been tiring, with tough ground and heavy-footed horses. Loreticus folded his wings back to fit through a door and the steep wooden steps beyond.

The stairs turned in on themselves, only wide enough for Marcan if he walked leading with his right shoulder. The poor light came from the stables below. It was reflected weakly by polished brasses on the walls, and was soon strengthened from a room above where a large door swung open, its dark wood and resplendent in the glow of dozens of tall candles.

Loreticus entered without a pause, stalking directly over to a robust older man, who was hoisting himself from a giant, heavily cushioned chair by the fireplace.

"Felix," declared Loreticus warmly, as they first clasped each other's forearms and then hugged.

"My old friend." Felix's voice was tenor and rough, as if he had been breathing this cold damp for all his life. He smiled as he watched Loreticus, examining him as a returning son. Marcan couldn't tell how much older he was than Loreticus, but he had always been useless with those native details. Instead, he captured the friendship between the men, the parity of thought, and he saw how his spymaster's face had melted into happiness. It was an expression that Marcan hadn't seen before.

Selban approached more discreetly, almost creeping across the floor with his sycophantic wobble. He smiled as a welcome to the old man, long before Felix even noticed him on the periphery of his conversation.

"And Selban," he greeted, again clasping forearms but foregoing the hug. There were few people in the country that dared to bring that pockmarked cheek close to their own. Peasant wisdom said that ugliness was catching, so beware who you marry and who you play with. No matter how elevated the palace walls, there was still such country chatter in the back of every courtier's mind. Felix studied Selban's face, before saying, "It seems you're on the mend. Are you still behaving yourself?"

"Of course, absolutely. All the time."

Felix smiled, turning back to Loreticus and gesturing to bring one of the other chairs nearer to the fire. Marcan looked around the room, a huge old hall which could have sat a small army. The rafters in the ceiling were ageless, and the wooden walls were stained and dirtied with soot, smoke, and the life of its inhabitants.

The old men had started talking and gave no indication to Marcan about what he should do. But before he committed himself to an introduction, he folded his arms and stared out of the window and listened to the rain as it grew heavier. Inside, against this warped glass, the drumming was friendly. The smell of dry old wood aflame in the hearth, the mixed warm and cool breezes of a cavernous room, the half-heard babble of older and wiser people. Marcan was visited by an intoxicating feeling of lost memories from a much younger self, sad and intimate. Something about how he felt now was too close to that same seclusion. It was comforting, hidden. He wasn't ready for whatever was next. Marcan took a deep breath, soaking in the vision of early night-time rain reuniting with a dry mountain pass, empty of people and talk. Then he turned, releasing the air methodically and quietly as he walked to the ingle.

Selban looked up and smiled, a genuine expression of delight at seeing Marcan, and gestured to his chair. Marcan shook his head, stepping nearer to Felix. His host looked up at him, and Marcan saw now the heavy bags under his eyes, the paleness of the blue in the gaze. Up close, he was more fragile, more decrepit. When he smiled however, even, white teeth gleamed.

"So, Marcan," he said, standing and grabbing his elbow, forcing him to clasp forearms. "You're my guest and my entertainment for the next few weeks, I understand. Fine, fine. We'll talk a lot and I'm sure you'll be able to enjoy some sleep." He looked again at Marcan's face, glancing at his chin, his cheeks, around his eyes. "You have something of the old boy himself," he said. He flung out an arm to the chairs in a manner which countered his earlier elegance before dropping into his own large, bum-beaten piece.

"Thanks, I'll stand by the fire," replied Marcan to the unspoken offer. "I've sat all day."

"Very wise," said Felix. "You don't want to end up like crooked Loreticus here." His eyes caught someone outside of the circle and he nodded. Shortly afterwards, breaking the silence that had tumbled, a middle-aged woman came with a generous wooden plate with roast meats and bread. Close up, the food looked delicious, perfect for the travellers after the ride and the rain. Somehow the echoing, empty hall stole the smells from the food. They ate in quiet, before Felix spoke. "You're going to see our zealous friends, are you?" He directed the question at Loreticus, as he chewed on a fat piece of white meat, his fingers holding it daintily between visits to his mouth.

Marcan paused, a pinch of bread halfway to his mouth. He didn't look up, but instead focussed on every word of this conversation. Loreticus was in league with the zealots?

Loreticus nodded. "We had to leave earlier than expected, so they need a little time to get things in shape." Selban peered sneakily at Marcan, excitedly hoping for some reaction to the news. Marcan ignored him. "But they are honest people."

"Ever the spymaster," muttered Selban in a jolly tone, milking the moment for its revelation. He was laughing directly at Marcan now.

"Kingmaker!" proclaimed Felix, lifting a finger demonstrably. "Better yet, kingdom builder!" He sniggered the way a fox coughed.

"Do be quiet," grumbled Loreticus with a pout. "I'm nothing of the sort. We've got problems and this man here is the only one with the true worth to fix things."

"But he needs more than that to be an emperor!" said Felix. "To be an emperor, he needs insight, foresight and wit. If he's anything like the old boy, he'll lack the lot."

"Who's the old boy?" asked Marcan, slightly unsettled by the conversation.

"The old emperor," replied Selban, pouncing on the closest thing to gossip he might find in the mountains.

"Felix was in his court for several years."

"He was a great man," stated Marcan by rote, for want of something to offer the watching faces.

"Nonsense. You barely knew him. He was a powerful man," said Felix. "Don't mistake the two." He turned to Loreticus, a tightness pulling his features together. "Your surprise arrival has its own risks," he said, more quietly this time. "I haven't had time to send my old maid away to make space for all of your people."

The spymaster stared at his host for a moment, the point of the comment obviously lost on him.

Then Loreticus made the connection and his face whitened. "Oh dear," he said and glanced instinctively, furtively at Marcan. His Adam's apple worked its way up and down his throat.

Marcan chewed his food slowly, waiting for something else to be said. He was lost. Loreticus was in bed with the zealots? He could cross the mountains? The subtle fiction that Marcan had built up since that first morning in Bistrantium felt a lot more fragile, a hubristic fantasy of a desperate man.

A paranoia tightened deep in his chest. He watched the logic of the situation unwrapping in its simple force as he stood before these three. Everything that he knew came from them. What had Alba told him, truly told him? Nothing but their own story.

These men had hidden him, keeping him from royal protection, and were now taking him to the zealots on the far side of the mountains. Demetrian guarded his exit but there must be another way out.

Loreticus dreamed of a unified kingdom, an empire

which encompassed the soldiers and the priests. For the spymaster and his gang to offer up a crucified emperor certainly flew the battle flag that he needed to lead the armies through the mountains.

As the realisation hit him, he felt a deep and shabby feeling of humility. Humility at his own incompetence, at the ease with which these veterans had pushed him off the throne. That destiny he had been bred and wed for, that role dozens of kings had filled comfortably before. He choked on the realisation that the entire court must have been behind this betrayal, laughing and plotting and lying, liaising even with the enemy to see it through. A pain in his chest grew as he realised that he was no more than a sacrificial lamb, fattened on ignorance and arrogance. His heart pulsated, and his lungs gulped air and his eyes sprung tears. Fear forced him to snap his head to look at the three men as he heard the scrape of their chairs on the floor.

"Grab him," shouted Felix and without warning Marcan's sight went black.

Words came to him and brought him back into the room. The smell of the log smoke, and two or three different conversations confused him; he kept his eyes closed as he tried to paint a picture of his surroundings.

"Fainted?" asked Selban's edgy voice.

"Collapsed," replied Loreticus.

The sound of people moving, the friction of their clothes creating a background. Felix said something to someone – by his voice Marcan presumed the lady that had served previously.

"Perhaps it is some long-term effect of the drug they gave him?" asked Felix curiously. No verbal answer came, but Marcan sensed that he had received a reply.

"Perhaps it is a simple weakness of mind," responded Selban in a tone that carried a deep disappointment.

Water splashed near his head, and he waited for a cloth or a press to placed on his brow but instead he heard someone pause.

"He's waking up," said the lady. It must have been his eyes rolling under their lids. He took a deep breath and came back to the room.

Five people stood in his line of sight–the three men, then Demetrian and the lady. She completed her chore, draping a cold, wet rag over his forehead and dabbing at his cheekbones with another. His skin felt dead, absent of sensation or movement. Somehow his hands were not his own, unresponsive and still. He accepted his incompetence and lay, rotating his gaze up to the massive rafters. He took the soft touch of his nurse, passive in her rhythmic patting.

"Do you need something, Marcan?" asked Felix. He could feel all their judgemental eyes on him, looking for a direction of his thoughts. The smallest gesture came from him, and he felt bizarrely that he might burst into a tight-faced crying fit. He pulled the rag down over his eyes and rolled his jaw, trying to regain control, certain that they could see through his charade.

"I'm going to bed," declared Loreticus. "I think we all should." Marcan listened to people turning, the wet towel still dabbing against his cheeks. "We'll see you before we go in the morning," he said to Marcan, and their footsteps moved away to the far end of the hall.

The lady remained.

"Who are you?" he whispered after a few minutes.

"Trudix," she replied, her voice strong and clean. "I live here with Felix." There was an educated, urbane accent, which was at odds with her current home. "You've had enough of their playing gods I should imagine. They've all disappeared off now."

He smiled to change the expression on his face.

"They are worried about you," she said and he felt the petulant urge to chastise her for her innocence.

"They are more worried about their politics," he grumbled. "I'm just their ransom."

"You shouldn't say that."

"I'm entitled to say that."

"Not when you're wrong," she castigated. "These four men all have their influence and authority. What they have in you, Marcan, is a leader by right and by talent."

"I think that you misunderstand," he replied.

"What do I misunderstand? That you don't know who you are, or that you don't think that you're ready for the throne yet?" She sounded smug in her rationale.

"I think that you misunderstand their plans for me."

"How so?"

"I don't think that I'm destined for the throne," he said. "I don't think that I'll be around long enough to even see the capital again." He opened his eyes, looking at her face for a response.

She was older, settled in her looks, seemingly happy.

"You'll see your family again," she replied. "Have some faith."

"I'm a broken man," Marcan said slowly. "Can I trust them?"

"Yes."

"Can I trust your judgement of them?"

Another laugh. "Yes, you can. I've always judged my husband and his friends more critically than anyone else."

They considered each other's faces for a moment, then he smiled purposefully.

"Thank you," he said. She nodded and put the rags in her wooden bowl.

Chapter 25

The hellish mountains bled into dry savannahs, and Loreticus felt relief and hope when he saw space. He felt he had made a pact with the mountains in exchange for their hospitality, and every crossing was to take a toll from his inner balance. When foothills came to a sudden stop, harder on this side than that of the empire, they cast a beautiful profile which belied their danger.

Ahead was Palova, the new capital of the religious territories. It was easy to enter; there was no major gate, no soldiers, no paranoia of imminent attack.

The city was still being built, a generation after its foundation. The roads ran straight into the centre, at which point the structure broke down into the sprawling chaos of the ancient trading town. Everywhere the architecture was the same: flat fronts with flat roofs, colourful doors the only sign of individuality. Sectors of the city were painted to reflect what types of buildings were allowed–blue for residential, red for trading, green for administration, yellow for the military. The streets were empty at this late hour and Loreticus rode slowly, the hooves of his horses clattering softly in a comfortable patter on the sandstone flags. He wore his hood down on his shoulders, as was the custom and the law in Palova.

A sloping, narrow path, so narrow that his tired and clumsy horse occasionally knuckled his knees on the sharp bricks, led him down to a nondescript arched door. This had retained the same colour as the walls–marine blue to three-quarters up the ground floor and then a lighter sky blue above, which ended unevenly as the second storey grew. He dismounted, stretched as much as he could and rapped on the door.

A spyhole slid open, followed soon after by the whole door. Before him stood a tall, stylish youth with a heavy moustache. His pale skin had absorbed the sun and shone golden, blending into a thin hairline high above a cultivated forehead. Blue eyes sparkled, white teeth quickly flashed and Loreticus was engulfed in a tight bear hug.

"My apostate friend!" roared the young man in a stage whisper. "So happy to see you! You're early."

This new accent always jarred unnaturally on Loreticus's old ears. It had been purposefully cultivated by the Palovans, worried about the lack of their own unique history. But there was something in their commitment to this accent, ugly as it was, that reflected their overall enthusiasm for life. They had created a community described only by superlatives amongst buildings of the deepest anonymity. It was the opposite of his home town. Just walking into Palova, Loreticus felt his emotions more readily and more deeply, as if a button had popped on his imperial costume.

"Javus," Loreticus returned warmly. He ignored a twinge in his back and simply squeezed his friend with all his strength. They stepped through the blue door, which led into a dishevelled courtyard with two doors, one for the house, and one to the household stable.

Javus turned and clicked his fingers twice. A small man came to his bidding, taking Loreticus's horse and leading it through to the stables. Loreticus had first been mildly shocked by the vicinity of the animals in the city, even though they slept in a different building. But after his first night in this chilly, half-built environment he realised that the animals acted as company, warmth and security. There was also a humility in their proximity which took away from the established order and compartmentalised lifestyle of the empire.

The other door was already open, and through it Loreticus could see the kitchen, the family table and a seating area at the far end. It was a linear, open room divided into three by narrow arches between columns, keeping the shape and atmosphere of the storage vault it had once been. Figures sat at the end, both female.

"Where's your father?" asked Loreticus.

"Out scaring the peasants," laughed Javus, flashing his big teeth again. Loreticus wondered how wide his smile was without that awful facial hair. They walked through the arches, Javus bolt upright whilst Loreticus dipped, constantly aware of the curves in the roof despite being shorter than his host.

"We have an apostate here," chuckled Javus, swinging his body to one side to reveal Loreticus to the others. Before him sat Javus's mother and sister, a woman without pretence or worry and her matching daughter. Unlike Javus, both were dark, with narrow noses and eyebrows that curved above happy, wise eyes. The mother rose, kissing Loreticus on both cheeks.

"You need tea, you poor man." She smiled.

"Thank you, I do. It's been a long ride and a longer season."

"I've heard. You must tell me everything when we are supping."

He sat down at a broad, round table which had an elaborate candlestick in its centre. The daughter pored over him, examining his pale face.

"So you're my brother's pet apostate?" she joked.

"And you're the zealot sister?"

She extended a hand. "Camina."

"Loreticus. And don't call me an apostate too quickly, my lady. I'm friends with my gods, but it's the men on this earth that I have issue with."

She exuded a confidence which he found refreshing and which was probably deserved. If she had the intellect which pervaded every other member of her family, then she was someone to pay attention to.

"Are you going to be getting my flighty big brother into trouble?"

"Very probably."

"Am I allowed to tell my father about your visit?"

"Um . . ." Loreticus looked to Javus, deferring the answer to him.

"I'll deal with Father."

Camina rolled her eyes. "Because you've had such a great success to date. Just let me know when you're going to 'talk' to him and I'll excuse myself to the library in advance."

They smiled at each other, a family joke.

Their mother sat down.

"Xania, how are you?"

"Very well, dear Loreticus." She leant over and wiped some dust from his tunic. "How long have you been travelling?"

"For a while," he said. "A brief stay before the mountains, but otherwise directly from the capital."

"Your capital," remarked Camina gently.

"Indeed," he chuckled. "The original capital."

"How is Felix?" asked Javus, pulling his moustache with his bottom lip.

"He's well," he replied. Javus had never met the old man, but he was one of the legends from the time of the exodus, or "Establishment" as they called it here. Javus wanted to be involved in something other than his modest life and for now he lived vicariously.

"How is our little prince?" asked Xania. Camina turned, showing more attention to this thread of conversation.

"Fine, although dazed and a little adrift," replied Loreticus. "But then I think we all are."

"It's healthy for him to get some of his own medicine," sniped Camina.

"Shut up, little sister," growled Javus. "You've got no idea of the background."

"How is this going to work?" asked Loreticus. "Camina here is not the only one in the house who we need to be wary of."

"Talio knows that we're expecting a guest and who it is." Xania looked calmly at Loreticus, who shook his head in shock. "He won't be a concern. He will abide by our religious code not to put a guest in peril."

"And as soon as your guest leaves the front door to go

back to assume the throne?"

"He'll be safe—you have my word," she said.

He couldn't challenge either Xania's belief or her honour. He had presumed that there was a hidden room or complex of rooms in which he could stow his contraband. He had tasks to perform in the capital without needing to worry about Marcan being strung up.

Loreticus stood.

"Sorry that my visit was so brief," he said. He registered their faces as they realised he was beginning to cut them out of his plans. "Javus, if I could ask a favour. I must get back now but my horse is spent. Could I take one of yours? It will be a more than fair swap, I promise."

"Of course," smiled Javus, quickly back in control. "Let me walk you to get prepared."

He let him say his farewells, then draped his arm over the older man's shoulders.

"Your temper might be the result of your hard journey or something else," started Javus.

"Temper, no. Sensible risk aversion is more like it. This isn't something that can go wrong."

"Let me finish. You forget a few simple things. You forget my father. His reputation as an angry man with a bloody blade is his public face. You know that. Nowadays, he's got stiff joints and he sees himself more as a persuader."

"He is an important man in a zealous country."

"He is a persuader," Javus repeated. "He will see—he sees—our guest as someone who should be talking with our leaders face to face. We need a truce. We live in constant fear that Iskandar or Ferran will come pouring out of the mountains with their cavalry one morning. It's the story we tell our children, our 'end of days'. This is my father's chance to create a strong link with the empire, not to make a demonstration."

"This is his chance to hold the empire to ransom."

"No." Again, Javus was gentle and calm. "I am not a religious man, you know that. I am here because my family is here. I am here despite my father. Why did I volunteer my home and my beliefs unless I thought it safe?"

They stood and watched Javus's horse being saddled. Loreticus turned and hugged his friend.

"I trust you," he said to Javus and examined his face as if remembering the details.

"I know," replied Javus. "You should."

"But I don't trust your logic, I'm sorry. Come to Felix's in a few days and I'll introduce you to him."

As he rode back out of the town, with night setting, the clouds darker than the sky behind them, Loreticus reflected on how some sons trusted their fathers too much. Every one of those three family members he felt a connection with and trusted on some level. But the family itself–the unit it created–he instinctively disliked and he didn't know why. Perhaps it was the father who poisoned the well. Perhaps they had grown twisted and knotted around his warped view of the world like the roots of an old tree around a broken fence. Whatever the cause, Javus was now the last resort for Marcan's sanctuary.

Chapter 26

"Did you trust your father, Marcan?" asked Felix.

"I honestly don't know."

The pair stood on the small mount behind the hall, watching Demetrian and his men run drills, cook, and groom their horses. Selban rarely rose from his bed before early afternoon and so Felix and Marcan had sat together through necessity rather than enthusiasm.

"I knew your father well and I didn't trust him at all. He was a predictable man, as most generals are, but he was a creature of his audience. He often agreed with the last person he spoke to. A disingenuous man," observed Felix.

"Why are you telling me this?"

"Because I was thinking about fathers today," he said somehow conveying a deep melancholy. "I got up, saw soldiers in my house with swords on their belts and felt ashamed. It took me a while to work out why but then I realised. My father always insisted that weapons be removed before people entered the house. It was such a rigid rule that even bodyguards had to abide by it. I quickly noticed that I was angry that these guests were wearing their weapons without a thought for my father's etiquette. That of course was swiftly followed by a sense of embarrassment." He spent a moment sucking something from between his grey teeth. "Fathers and childhoods leave long, shadowy legacies. Your father was a manipulator and I wonder how much of him is in you."

"I am completely my father," replied Marcan calmly. He wanted to somehow shock this arrogant old man who thought he could insult his late father. "Of course, I am. But I'm not dishonest or scheming, if that's what you are so bluntly implying. I'm my own person who has lost more battles than he has won. I am a simple wooden figurehead for the likes of Loreticus and Selban to play around with."

"Oh, I'm not saying that," interrupted Felix. "You're still the emperor, albeit in exile. You're still married to the imperial daughter and you're still the ruling head of the country."

"So I'm nice and valuable for Loreticus and his chums."

"And you think that you are better off with the generals?"

"Wouldn't you, if you were in my shoes?" He gestured to the damp scrublands around the base of the cold mountains. "Hardly a triumphant return for a lost emperor."

"True. But you owe your life to Loreticus. You know that?"

"No, I don't," muttered Marcan petulantly. "There are two scenarios in my mind. Either he screwed up and let me get into this mess, or he is not sharp enough to influence a headstrong emperor. Either way he doesn't look like a success."

"You'd be a peasant actor still without him," said Felix. "You know, one trick that you should have learned on stage was honesty. Once you've learned to fake that, you can be an actor or a politician." Felix took a deep breath in, and Marcan understood it to be a judgement of his poor character. "Loreticus is far too keen to play jigsaws with other people's lives, and we let him. His brains and his charm are his downfall in this respect because no-one challenges the value of his plans or their logical outcome. He's the best you've got, mind."

"I'm fairly sure that the only person I need is Demetrian. He's the action to Loreticus's warbling. I certainly don't owe my life to Loreticus," he repeated.

"Why don't you like him?"

"I don't like schemers," Marcan said flatly.

A pause. Marcan didn't like the subject of the conversation. They were a breath away from discussing the blood soaked return to the throne that they had planned over those rough peaks.

"Which drug did they give you that night you didn't shag the girl?"

"I don't know. I didn't wait around to chat with her."

"So you think that she did it? Not a slave's sleight of hand and the Lady Iskandar was an innocent bystander?"

Marcan observed him. His change in posture must have already signalled to Felix that he disliked him and the conversation that he was forcing.

"I don't hold to that theory."

"Which? The guilty slave?"

"No."

"Why not?"

"It implies that Dess was there with other intent than to create a damning scene. That implies my guilt somehow."

"Which is?"

"That she and I were involved." Marcan stood. His chest was getting tighter, his breathing shallower and he needed to suck in the dank mountain air to fill his dry airways. It was dawning on him that perhaps his confusion before his fall from grace had not been an unintentional distraction. Perhaps it was his own quiet mind making sure that he never attempted to fill a role for which he was unqualified. That was ever more the case now.

Perhaps his dislike for Loreticus was based on the fact that the old man could read him so easily. He could command immediate obedience from anyone around him, with that devilish smile and smooth charm, or the frightening ice that lay in his blue eyes. What kind of man denied himself the throne when he had such tangible power? A schemer. A puppet master, making Marcan the puppet.

"There's another issue which is concerning," stated Felix in an unnaturally informal tone, typical of a pompous advocate anticipating the deadly blow to his opposite's logic. He waited for a prompt, bringing his companion back on to his ground.

"And what is that?" Marcan asked, forcing civility into his tone.

"I don't know of any drug which has such a strong effect as the poison did on you. Normally you are knocked out for a night or a day perhaps, but after you wake up you have only lost that time during which you were unconscious. To lose your own name seems severe."

"Your point?"

"Do you think that witchcraft was involved?"

The suggestion was mocking and Marcan wondered again about the old man's agenda.

"I didn't realise that you knew the details of every drug in the world in every different mixture," his words laced with sarcasm.

"Oh, I don't," replied Felix. "You're right. I'm stuck up here and might well have missed a new concoction."

"I need to piss," Marcan said. He stood up and started walking down the slope.

"You can piss here," called the old man.

"No," came back the reply.

Marcan had not been in the company of such a wealth of intellect before, and it challenged his idea of his own destiny. He had an unshakeable distrust of these people, and this clawed at the idea that he had been given a purpose by the world. Would the gods have chosen such a bunch of creepy, conniving men who revelled in their own sordid natures? He gave credit to Balthasar for his portrayal of this wretched political class.

In front of him, Pello dashed around the side of the smaller building, which had housed the various domestic staff when this estate had housed a grander generation. Marcan felt a heave of gratitude when he saw the boy, blond hair bouncing as he moved in his half-walk, half-trot, his uneven eyes fixed on a thought which seemed to run a few steps in front of his own toes on the ground.

Pello looked up as Marcan's footsteps reached him. He froze, stared at his face, turned to look in panic over his shoulder, then swung his panicked expression back to Marcan.

A sickly sensation ran through Marcan, an angrier, more vengeful version of the emotion which had felled him on his first night. Rage burned up his sternum, conquering the reason in his head, and with a dramatic lurch, he galloped forward, past the now scampering Pello towards the hidden plotters behind the corner of the cottage wall. He could not stand anymore to have these arrogant old men talking behind his back, planning his future for him.

As he approached, he could see a blurred shadow in the pallid sunshine and he bunched his fists, content to let his mouth utter whatever flew from it before his reactions caught up.

Two steps, one step and he barrelled around the corner. He blinked several times, wondering whether his mind had cracked again.

Loreticus and Selban weren't there, plotting and scheming with bloodied knives and poison pouches around them. Instead, an old lady sat, rocking in an ancient, beaten chair, its arms so old that the wood was polished from a million touches.

She looked up and saw him. They stared. He hadn't seen this face for a long time, but he remembered her perfectly, the first face he ever remembered seeing. The crone from the marketplace in Bistrantium.

Chapter 27

Eduus was the assassin of choice in the generals' circles. He was precise and lithe, full of a wry humour and the edgy arrogance of a diminutive man.

Eduus designed his own cloth-soled shoes and he was rather proud of them. After this big payoff, he would hire apprentices to make them for him. He could sell them to soldiers and mercenaries and make a healthy income which would be better to live on than his retainer from Flaky Ferran.

Three knives of different sizes were smothered in his belt and across his back. Each was sharpened to a butcher's perfection–after all, cutting through skin was as tough as cutting through pig hide. He was a proud man, making sure that his hair was cut and his nails were buffed before an exercise like this one. He figured that if the details were planned and prepared, then luck was on his side.

Eduus had slogged all the way from the border to this pair of ramshackle huts, following the tracks of horses which rode in semi-military style. The horses were well-shod, which implied a wealthy set of riders. One day, they would teach his tracking skills in the military academy, revelling in his powers of deduction.

The problem before him was the clear space between the break of the slope up to the plateau and the buildings. He presumed that the guard who was making his fire outside the hall front was the only one out, as was the standard military procedure in this situation. Against an attacking force, why expose the squad when they just needed one man to make a noise? He waited, hands down the front of his trousers to keep them warm, watching the shadows around the hall corners and the sides of the smaller house. After half an hour, Eduus raised himself into a stoop and trotted noiselessly across the open ground, then dropped flat on his belly. His green and grey clothes kept him as a shadow against the floor, breaking up his silhouette. He repeated the procedure and pressed himself against the cold floor again, sure that the guard must have been able to hear his breathing. Nothing. The man was sitting, watching the fire, complacent in his reverie.

Eduus lay sprawled, wondering how to attack without raising the alarm. He was lucky that the clouds had quenched the moonlight and he had been able to get this close, but he was still stuck in a dilemma between a rapid attack and patience. A stealth attack was as likely to cause a shout of shock as a raised blade, and that was worse in this situation. Eduus trusted himself to make the right choice when it became clear. Whenever he felt unsure, he reminded himself that he was the imperial choice–the best in the land.

Then his luck changed. The guard stood up, towering a lot taller than Eduus had expected, left his helmet by the fire and stepped slightly away, unlacing the front of his trousers. A noise of piss thumping against the rocky earth and the soldier's released breath. One step, two steps and then a short sprint. Eduus jumped, his left hand grappling the mouth shut and lifting the jaw. His knife peeled open the throat with such a wide stroke that it burst the veins on either side. Teeth bit hard into the tough leather on the inside of his fingers, wisely gloved against puncture. As the soldier sagged, he shrank and Eduus's feet came back into contact with the ground. He gently helped the big man down before turning to the main building.

Marcan had planned his escape that afternoon as he listened to Felix natter on. The original architect of the manor house had made the windows small to prevent entry from any average-sized attacker.

But he had walked the perimeter of the building and he had found what he was looking for, something every residence in the empire had. And so, after the sun had fallen and the party had dispersed, Marcan slipped out of the hall door. Down the spiral steps, as quietly as he could manage, given his nerves. His presumption was that his hosts' horses were stabled in the smaller building as none were with Demetrian.

At the bottom of the narrow staircase, a door stood open and Marcan could hear the guards chatting and detect the smell of hot wine. Further down he went, following these age-old steps in to the guts of the house. Something cracked in front of him, and he stiffened. There were no torches down the stairs, and the only light came from the open door above. He crouched silently, wanting to minimise any silhouette. Something small moved away from him down the steps and he had the impression that he had not been seen.

Further down, the light vanished and he crouched again, waiting for his night eyes to come to him. He could feel on his cheeks a dryness from his surroundings, and there was a smell of old wood. Marcan advanced, hesitantly stretching his fingers in front of him to get a bearing. After a few steps, he felt a stack of something and guessed fire logs. Further into the darkness he went, praying that his inner compass was leading him to the half-hidden trap door at the side of the house.

Eduus crept around the base of the building and after two circuits found the trap door for the wood. With his fingertips, he traced the edges and stepped back to find something to pry it open. As he squinted in the dark, he missed the trap slowly opening of its own volition.

He turned back to see a heavy silhouette emerge from the edge of the house. Not usually a superstitious man, this apparition was more than enough to give him pause. Then the shadow froze as it saw Eduus and the spell broke.

The assassin charged into action, stepping forward heavily and whipping his hand back and forth, launching a line of wicked knife blades. Two struck – he could tell by the movement of the shadow – but the last bounced off the wall behind him.

Then the shadow was moving silently, murderously closer to him. He was fast and he caught Eduus with a blistering punch across his ear. The assassin tumbled, shocked but somehow ready. Out came two of the small blades again, one still dirty with the guard's flesh. Eduus threw a flurry of jabs, some killing shots, others to distract. But the man ducked and bobbed, and in the dark Eduus couldn't find the strike that he wanted.

Then the shadow came into the moonlight and the assassin paused. Standing, bloodied and furious in front of him, was the Emperor Marcan. No more than half a heartbeat and the routine started again, but this time the assassin knew that he had lost the advantage.

Marcan came, his fists drilling into open ribs and unprotected face. Then the emperor lost his footing in the fresh mud, his body slipping, and Eduus's blade dug through his clothes and stuck in the flesh low down on his rib cage.

Marcan snarled, slapped Eduus with an open palm which felt like rock. It stunned the assassin, rocking him backwards. Marcan half tumbled, half staggered to the shadows. A noise of a fall and Eduus lost sight of him.

He ducked, checking for movement and then closed in. The trap door was closed tight. Eduus stooped, snatching up the two fallen knives on the ground and arranged himself. He was breathing heavily, nursing a split lip and the side of his head felt red hot from the bruising that was coming. But he was close, and his knife was sitting between the emperor's ribs. His professional pride now demanded proof of the kill.

Something told him that Marcan wouldn't raise the alarm. The man looked like he had been trying to sneak away, not hide, so Eduus hunted again for a way in. A window was open near the far end. It would be a scramble to get in, but he was much smaller and slighter than the average person. Eduus sprinted on his cloth feet, listening for any change in the sounds around him. One, two, then he launched again, catching the edge of the window with his fingertips so that he couldn't be seen from inside. Gently he raised his eyes above the mantle. Perfectly quiet, his muscles honed and responsive despite the long journey, the thrill of the murder and the cold heightening every movement.

Nothing inside to worry about. The servants' kitchen, it appeared. A brace of half-butchered rabbits lay on one counter to his left, and to the right the room spread out of his view. The light was not strong, although coming in from the dark it was as blinding as the sun. He heaved himself through the aperture and landed as gently as he could. Something crackled, then popped. He took another step, the floor feeling uneven under his soft-soled shoes. It gave way with a scratching noise and then a crack.

Another noise and all of a sudden Eduus found himself bathed in light. In front of him, a guardsman rolled over to look at who had made the noise. Eduus glanced down at the floor, where broken crockery had been scattered as an early-warning trap.

The guard yelled at the top of his lungs, and Eduus stepped forward to drive the heel of his clothed foot into the man's open jaw. In the sudden silence, he could hear movement catalysed by the alarm. Eduus wheeled, not daring to look behind him, and dashed on to the table and back through the window.

Chapter 28

Loreticus woke as his door opened, and he watched the shape of Demetrian move into his room. The soldier sat quietly in a chair against the wall.

"What happened?"

"An assassin. He killed two of my men – one outside and one downstairs. We didn't catch him, so he's gone back to his masters."

Loreticus sat up, the warmth from under his blankets now seeping off him. He rubbed his eyes, stood, smoothed his hair back then started dressing.

"I presume that you've checked on Marcan?" he asked in the dark.

"Yes," replied Demetrian. "A strange situation there. He had a knife in his ribs – nothing serious as it caught on the bindings of his cuirass. It gave him a nasty scratch, but nothing life-threatening."

"The assassin got that far?"

"No, he didn't. By my logic, Marcan went to meet him. Something went wrong and Marcan escaped back in to the house. I found blood from the trap door to the cellar to his bed."

"What did he say?" Loreticus was incredulous now,

standing with a boot hanging from one hand. "Was he trying to escape back to the capital?"

"Nothing. He simply made it understood that questions were not welcome. Stuck his bottom lip out as usual."

"You should have made him talk!" growled Loreticus as an anger spilled in to his mind. The damned fool could do nothing easily. Was it something with the leaders in this empire that they tried every stupid option until all that was left was the obvious one?

"Loreticus, let me remind you – Marcan is my emperor. You are not."

The party gathered in the great hall, which was lit only by the refuelled fire in the hearth. As Loreticus entered, no-one was talking. Marcan stood, eyes down, a hand on his side. Selban watched the emperor's face, occasionally glancing at Loreticus to gauge the dynamic. Felix sat by the fire, and Trudix stood on her own as if to watch the entire scene. Both still wore their bed clothes. By the door to the stairs Demetrian waited, flanked on either side by guards dressed in their riding armour.

"We've been betrayed," stated Loreticus. He folded his arms, then considered Marcan. "The generals know that we're here. You're a dead man if we stay; you're a dead man if we go back to the capital. We only have one direction to go."

"Palova," said Felix. He matched Marcan's silent look. "We have friends in the highest places there. Friends that will look after you and will keep you safe."

"The mountains are horrible. They are impossible for a convoy, and coming down into the zealots' countryside as a group is waving a flag," Loreticus stated to Demetrian. "Therefore, you will escort the emperor and myself to just before mid-way. Marcan and myself will go on alone from there."

Loreticus could see in the soldier's expression that he was not happy with the decision, but Loreticus's word held. No-one in that room but Loreticus had crossed the mountains. The great peaks inspired an otherworldly fear in the empire's soldiers, and Loreticus drew on that now. He had conquered the mountains, not once but several times. What reputation he had once commanded during the Terror had multiplied amongst those who knew him over the years. That Loreticus could perform an awe-inspiring act did not instill confidence that others might match him.

"Everyone should be ready to leave immediately. Demetrian, you are responsible for getting the emperor out of the door and on a horse pointing in the right direction."

"Yes, Loreticus."

The spymaster paused, wanting to say something more, but simply turned and walked back in the direction of his room. Slowly Selban and Felix left their positions until only the soldiers at the door accompanied Marcan and Trudix.

She moved over to him and laid a hand on his arm.

"Don't judge us all for the chaotic world we live in," she said. "If you did, then you'd only be underestimating the wilfulness of your enemies." He considered her, wondering how to respond. She smiled. "Get packed, follow Demetrian and then Loreticus. Just don't hurt them and don't hurt yourself."

She left him in the glow of the fire, walking back to the bedrooms.

Loreticus watched her approach and saw her startled expression when she saw him in the dark.

"Bloody spymasters," she said with a smile.

"What do you think, Trudix?" he asked.

"I don't know. I want to trust him but he makes it hard."

"Should we force him in to this, or should we let him go and let the empire do what it needs to do? I honestly don't know why I'm fighting so hard for a man without loyalty or brains."

"You're too hard on him, Loreticus," she said. "He's intelligent but you've always disliked people who disagree with you. On this occasion, force him. But just remember that he might hold it against you for a long time."

"Then why do it?"

"Because you will have to fight many battles to win a war. Take the easier decisions lightly," she said.

Chapter 29

The sun came up cold on the travellers, its white light icier than the moon behind them. The steppes sharpened and bristled on its arrival, as they had every morning for thousands of years. And so it was with dread that Loreticus left Selban, Demetrian and the guard at the edge of the higher peaks, and went forward alone with Marcan to Palova.

Neither spoke as they moved forward, Marcan turning back once to see the line of men blocking the path to the capital.

Loreticus watched the young man as their horses padded through the chill air. The original Marcan had been married less than two years. How could a man who had been so well groomed and so well bred have caused so much damage within those few months?

Marcan had to encourage his mount on to the dirty snow which crept down from its settling place higher up the grey slopes. Underfoot it was unsound, patchy ice turning into a thick, greasy rug, the hard hooves of the horses whisking away under their own weight. In front of them stretched a bleak, dirty valley of untrodden snow, broad and flat swathes waiting with an unfeeling mastery.

Loreticus wrapped a fur cloak around his shoulders, inwardly grunting under its weight. To his satisfaction, Marcan looked uncomfortable as well with his broad shoulders curled into his chest, his chin down. This was a side to the young ruler that no-one else saw, thought Loreticus. Sullen, childish, dependent.

The route through the Border Mountains took two days, possibly three if the best passes were closed. Soon there would be a necessity to carve through this rock and to build a road. The zealots had broken its back and a tentative black market was beginning to establish itself between the communities. Loreticus had often marvelled how close the new territories were. Marcan's integrity, if he ever took the throne again, would be sorely tested once he realised just how unguarded Palova was.

The first night was the hardest because of the recent comfort of a fireplace and warm food. Their minds were still alert and it felt awkward ignoring each other, but they both succeeded in doing so. Neither slept comfortably, but Marcan couldn't complain because this was a journey the older man had made several times on his own. Despite his deep dislike of Loreticus, Marcan began to regard him with more respect.

Exhaustion conquered their discomfort the second night. They slept, as did their horses and mules. Silence was easier now. It was a routine.

The final night was simple. Although the thick ice had gone, cold rain came down hard, whipping diagonally across them as if the mountains were taking their last chance to inflict hurt. Before they lit the fire, which they lidded with a pot, Marcan saw a pool of light at the end of the pass. It was there briefly, then the rain came again and closed his first glimpse of the distant Palova.

The morning brought surrender, or at least a ceasefire, from the mountains. Sunlight pushed back the wet, and the snow became infrequent underfoot. The beasts even gave an occasional snort or nervous bite of excitement as they saw the land fall warm and flat in front of them.

But Loreticus could see the cold still haunted Marcan. His eyes were frozen and his pinched lips remained blue after their cloaks were flung over the horses' flanks.

The storm clouds that appeared to be permanently in the mountains when seen from the capital were now seen to be hovering on the other side of the plateau. They were majestic, huge, rolling within themselves.

"I always thought that they sat on top of the Border Mountains," said Marcan.

"They most often do. They've obviously taken a tour of the valley in your honour."

"How do you do that journey?" asked Marcan. "It's bone breaking."

"I've only gone through the mountains a few times. But when you know what to expect, it's no worse than when I was fighting the barbarians in my youth. In those days, instead of mountains, it was frozen forests. You remember habits, manage your thoughts."

"No wonder you're such a melancholy bastard."

"That's more to do with my current employment," replied Loreticus. He felt that Marcan's forced familiarity was unnecessary. There was nothing between them now other than duty, and so there was no reason to engage. Loreticus wondered why he had expected a different relationship with his emperor just because he had saved him.

"Don't you think that my return is a cause for joy?"

"If you get through this, then probably. If we must slog it out for another year, then maybe. If the zealots get massacred by you or the boneheaded generals, or taken back as slaves, then no."

Marcan ignored him and stared out, squinting at the city in front of them.

"It doesn't look much."

"It's different. It's growing fast." He paused. "Unlike our capital, this is a city made beautiful by its people more than its buildings."

"Where will you go if you have to run into exile?"

"Here, I suppose," replied Loreticus. "Then Surran, then beyond the water. Why? Planning your contingency?"

"Loreticus, you think that I owe you a lot so I'll be honest. Desertion from my fate is likely to be my first choice. You, Selban and Demetrian, and certainly Darcy, have a clear idea of who an emperor is. I've failed once, despite the advantages I was given. I'm as likely to fail again. Add on to that a reward for my death, two countries chasing me and a wife who will judge me for the rest of my life, and I don't feel that going back offers me anything other than unhappiness."

"Well," replied Loreticus with a smile. "You do have a few challenges. But at least you can count them, whereas many people don't want to understand what's making them sad. No-one is happy, they'll say. Life is not perfect." He prodded a finger towards Marcan. "But you, my poor little runaway, you have a unique potential to make it better for thousands of people. If you don't squander it again. Just remember that you'll always be lonely, no matter what you do. Running or leading, neither can be done in partnership. Anyway, I heard that you were a poor actor."

"Maybe I can sing," replied Marcan.

"No, you can't. I'm surprised your memory loss allowed you the luxury of forgetting that."

"Well then, old man, what do you want from me? A simple puppet or a sacrificial offering to get your politicking ways?"

"No. I want an emperor. My country, the one I've lived in since birth, the one my family lived in, the one I've served for all my adult life, needs a strong emperor. You have it inside you. We're all idiots for the first half of our lives until we're not. I don't want the soil my wife and child are buried in to change. I buried them well. Forgetting the glory and the promise of the capital is forgetting them."

"You can't put that on me."

"I can and I have. You can have a little more time to wallow in your weakness, but you need to grow up fast. You can be an idiot, but you are the most intelligent man I know most of the time."

"Then how come I'm here?" asked Marcan.

"Because you're not always intelligent." Loreticus pushed his unfinished food away. "I don't trust you, Marcan. It isn't your motives, or your intellect that I have difficulties with. It's your common sense. It's your dislike of loyalty, either being loyal or trusting people. You've always had this flighty behaviour and it's causing me, us, your wards, untold damage. I don't believe that you betrayed us at Felix's. I think that you were about to do something foolish, but the others believe that you have sold out to the generals. Much as you like to think yourself a man, you act like an adolescent."

Marcan stared at his food.

"I don't trust you, Loreticus," he said slowly. "I can't understand you. I don't understand why you don't take the throne and run the country as you see fit. It feels illogical of you to fight for me to win the throne."

"I don't take that power, Marcan, for many, many reasons. The first is that I am a man of tradition, and the throne is yours. What does that say about me if I stab someone in the back for passing glory? Another reason is simply that I don't like people overall. Other than circuits at parties and court visits, I prefer my old friends."

"Why?" asked Marcan. "What have you got to hide?"

"As much as anyone else. But it's not that. It's how these common people ask about personal issues, and that's exactly what I'm trying to forget." He sucked in a deep, angry breath through his nose. "No. Let me do my good work, then let me rest. I don't care for another man to judge me."

Marcan stared at him.

"I was asking about the throne, not someone's judgement."

"You were asking too much," stated Loreticus and stood up to pack his food supplies away.

The downward slope and the sight of buildings spurred the horses' gait. They made the edge of the small city by mid-afternoon.

"Don't talk," Loreticus instructed. Marcan had infected him with doubt and this link in the whole chain, this evening's activities were the weakest of his whole plan. Walking the exiled emperor into enemy territory, to the very home of the man who had been the most brutal separatist of the zealots. "Don't wear your hood. In fact, change already into the clothes I gave you. Remember to put a dot of blue dye between your brows occasionally. Plead ignorance quite openly and say you came into the city from a farmstead."

"You do know that you've told me this many, many times before?" asked Marcan, seeing the old man's nerves.

"Yes, but remember you have a poor memory."

When they stopped for a short, warm supper, they both changed into blue clothes and marked their brows with the dye. The horses were tired and fidgeted with their saddles when the riders were off.

"Maybe it will keep me honest," chuckled Marcan. His humour had returned with the warmth of the town.

"Maybe. But maybe you keep yourself safe and hidden away until I come back."

"And when will that be, Loreticus?" Marcan offered his cupped hands for Loreticus's knee as he mounted. Loreticus didn't look at him but took the help.

"I don't know. Soon. I need to understand what we should do next."

"Shouldn't I be involved in that?"

"No, not now."

"Keeping me hidden away is not going to improve that situation. You realise that if you want me to be the emperor, I need to understand the responsibilities? Perhaps I should order you to include me."

"Firstly, you were once an emperor with a big mouth and secondly, try enforcing that instruction whilst you're stuck eating flatbread on the wrong side of the mountains."

"I do worry you don't respect me enough sometimes, old man."

"Well, that's because at this moment in time you're bloody useless. You've made some incredibly bad choices, so why should I cross the mountains to get your approval every time I need to act? Your job is to be quiet and to stay strong for the next month or so. My job is to fix a broken throne."

Marcan watched him for a moment. The sun was colder here, but the grass and the flowers smelled fresher. A citric fragrance surrounded them, small flies hovering low as the air sank for the night.

"Where is it you care for me? Is it in your head, your heart or simply because you don't like the other option? It seems between me and the other three monkeys, I am the best of a bad choice."

"Why do you care?" said Loreticus, then regretted his surliness. "Maybe there is a lot of truth in what you say. I didn't like the person you were, but I am loyal to the man before you and to your wife. I am hoping you'll be a better man than you were before you left the palace in the spring."

"Why help me at all? Why you, Loreticus? You could go away and live your years out."

"Because," said Loreticus, "one day, several years ago, I made a promise to a mother and son that I shall make this kingdom safe and quiet. A place where children smile every day, where families are safe because violence has no place in its streets. I have certain options to get to my goal. But I have no options about whom to sit on the throne."

"I don't know how to feel about that."

"You don't have to feel anything," said Loreticus, cold once more. "I'll give you your throne back and I'll give you a safe country. You simply need to follow the breadcrumbs." Loreticus gave his famous smile once more, but there was a coldness in the expression. He had lost none of his suave manner, and his voice contained little anger or frustration.

Quiet again. Whatever friendship Marcan considered forging with Loreticus had dissipated. There was nothing between them but a shared destiny, and Marcan was tired of being blamed for a different man's mistakes. He hadn't asked for the details of what had happened to make this old man so bitter. It was not his fault, not his problem.

"So what happens if the old Marcan comes back?"

"He won't. You're a changed man," stated Loreticus flatly. "Or are you implying that you're not the real Marcan?"

"And what if I'm not the real Marcan? What if I'm a fraud?"

"If you mean another claimant might arrive, then think back to what I want. A worthy emperor is preferable to a legitimate one."

The horses sluggishly lifted their hooves again, disgruntled at their being ridden further at the end of a long day.

"At least come back in a fortnight to keep me up to speed."

"I expect to, dependent upon how passable the mountains are and how paranoid the generals."

"Loreticus," said Marcan, "I'm your emperor."

"No. You're not yet."

AUTHOR'S NOTE

Thank you for reading LORETICUS, the first book in the Lost Emperor Trilogy series. I hope that it offered some escape and some inspiration in its pages.

My vision for this story partly came from a boardroom struggle to which I was a close witness. It struck me that it was a timeless story. That was the plot.

The setting was originally an exploration of the India–Pakistan separation. I read about how the difference in beliefs and cultures drove the segregation of the countries, but of course the functions of the original state didn't split as evenly. The army was very much Pakistani in its roots, and so when the smaller country formed it found itself with a large military machine to support. This has caused troubles since; every government needs to win the support of the generals before they win control of the country.

In the Lost Emperor trilogy I cheat and use an alternative historical setting, a fictional world based on Rome. Were I to have used Rome in its true form, the details of how the characters interacted with their environment would have been of greater importance than the plot in my mind. I was keen to divorce from this historical legacy, but keep its splendor. Better I focus on the exchanges of imperfect information between the characters in the book, than the imperfect knowledge of real history by the author and/or the reader.

Instead I concentrated on the patchwork of stakeholders, each with their ambitions and desires. This plot is drawn straight from real life (excluding the occasional assassination and use of poisons). As a soldier without a general in that particular fight, it was a fascinating and troubling series of episodes for me to watch.

Loreticus continues his struggle to put his candidate back on the throne in the next book in the trilogy, THE BATTLE OF PALOVA, in which he brings the generals face to face on the battlefield. The final episode, THE SETTLEMENT OF SURRAN, concludes the Loreticus trilogy as the empire unwittingly bursts its borders.

You can sign up for free pre-release orders via the mailing list at www.loreticus.com (limited numbers each month), as well as receiving free exclusive content such as the play script, maps and character backgrounds.

J.B. Lucas

LORETICUS RETURNS IN THE BATTLE OF PALOVA

Chapter 1

She measured her toes against the mock battlements on the edge of the roof and looked out over her final sunset. Below her, the palace gardens reached in etched detail to the thick walls. Miniature soldiers marched along them, slow and relaxed in their routines. Elma was a tall lady, handsome in an unusual way which her brother told her was unique and charming. She felt nothing of the sort. She felt, gangly and stretched. Too tall for a woman and too gentle for her height. Not in his eyes though. Elma could make him and his friends laugh with her wit when she knew them well, and she would lead a stylish dance with any who dared when the music arose.

So it was a pleasant relief that she felt the good moments in her soul as she stepped over. Not the embarrassment, or the loss. The certainty that she would be back with her brother and father very soon. As the grand red tower sped past her, windows and gargoyles blurring past, she fell in full control of herself.

With a soft crack her body landed with tremendous speed in to the rose garden at the base of the tower. A small garden accessed by only one door at ground level and one master door to the tower. Guards rarely came in here, even more rarely visitors. This was the spymaster's tower and this was Elma's only chance to ensure that he understood the importance of her message.

HELP LORETICUS ON HIS JOURNEY

Reviews on Amazon, Goodreads, Kobo and B&N are the single most important way for debut authors to build their readership. If you enjoyed LORETICUS, and think that at least one other person might while away a few hours enjoyably in these pages, please leave a short sentence saying as much.

Made in the USA
Middletown, DE
02 September 2017